HILDEGARD HODG.   ; author and
illustrator, she was edu   rammar School in
Bradford, West Yorkshir.

   She has travelled exte.   uved in New Zealand for
several years. Now retired, s   es with her husband in North
Yorkshire.

THE STRANGE INSIDE WORLD OF THE NIBBY NABBIES

THE STRANGE INSIDE WORLD
OF THE NIBBY NABBIES

Hildegard Hodgson

ATHENA PRESS
LONDON

ISBN: 978 1 84748 344 7

First published 2008 by
ATHENA PRESS
Queen's House, 2 Holly Road
Twickenham TW1 4EG
United Kingdom

Printed for Athena Press

This book is for Frances, my fearless granddaughter

CONTENTS

Part One

An Unexpected Adventure

It was a lovely sunny afternoon.

Francesca and her best friend Isabella were allowed by their parents to have a picnic on the beach.

'Here is your picnic hamper,' said Francesca's mummy, 'and I have put in a torch for each of you. Now go off and enjoy yourselves, and don't forget to stay well away from the water's edge.'

Carrying their hamper between them, Francesca and Isabella wandered down a pleasant country lane until they reached a lovely beach.

'Look over there,' said Isabella, pointing to a large group of rocks, 'I think that could be the place for our picnic.'

Just as Francesca and Isabella had settled down to enjoy themselves, a huge dark cloud appeared above their heads.

'Come on, Isabella, let's run and shelter in one of those caves before it rains!'

Picking up their hamper, the two girls ran across the beach as fast as they could, and ducked into one of the many caves just in time before a heavy downpour of rain began.

'Phew, that was close!' said Francesca. 'Another second or two and we would have been wet through. Come on, let's explore this cave and see if there is anything in it.'

Taking their torches from the picnic hamper, Francesca and Isabella set off down the cave. As the light began to fade, the girls switched on their torches and shone the beams of light around the cave.

They could see thousands of tiny bones and skulls.

'I wonder where they have come from,' whispered Isabella.

'They might have been washed up by the sea,' said Francesca.

Little did the girls know, further inside in the cave, a Giant Crab was hiding under the sand. He was there to guard the entrance, and to make sure that no humans from the Outside World entered the Inside World.

However, as Francesca and Isabella got closer to the crab, the giant creature, having never seen humans from the Outside World before, and not quite knowing how to deal with them, quickly buried himself deeper into the sand.

Within a few steps of where the Giant Crab lay hidden, the girls entered a large cavern, illuminated by the glimmer of many thousands of glow-worms that hung down from the roof of the cavern.

This was the very first time that any humans had entered the Inside World of the Nibby Nabbies.

Gazing round, Francesca and Isabella saw lots of tunnels leading out of the cavern.

'What has happened?' whispered Isabella. 'A moment ago we were at the back of a cave, and now we are in this huge, silent cavern!'

'I don't know,' said Francesca, 'but let's go back; I don't like this place.'

Turning round, the girls suddenly found that they could go no further.

'That's strange,' said Isabella. 'We came in this way, but we cannot get back out.'

Francesca and Isabella had entered the Inside World of the Nibby Nabbies through the Invisible Wall of No Return.

Try as they might, the girls could find no escape.

'What can we do to get out of here?' whispered Isabella to Francesca.

'I think the only way would be to make our way down one of those tunnels. Come on, let's give it a try,' said Francesca.

As they made their way across the sandy cavern floor, eyes

were observing them from behind and under the rocks that were strewn all over the cavern floor. There were many creatures watching, but they did not dare come out from their hiding places: they had never seen humans before and were very afraid.

In the eerie silence of the cavern, Francesca and Isabella approached the entrance to one of the many tunnels.

'It's pretty dark in there,' whispered Isabella.

'Let's switch our torches on and see where it leads,' said Francesca.

Shining their torchlights into the darkness of the tunnel, they saw lots of small snakes, lizards and beetles slither and scuttle away into cracks and holes in the sides of the tunnel wall.

'Those creatures live in total darkness, and don't like any light at all. They won't hurt us. Come on, Isabella,' said Francesca, 'let's be brave and keep walking.'

After what seemed a very long time, Francesca and Isabella came to the end of the tunnel, and walked into a Great Chamber.

Looking round it by the shimmering lights from the glow-worms, Francesca and Isabella could see a long platform against the wall of the Great Chamber.

On the platform was a chair with many carvings of reptiles, and laid across the arms of the chair was a broomstick. In very neat rows, hundreds of tridents were placed on the smooth, sandy floor. Francesca and Isabella had entered the Great Chamber of the evil, ancient, cackling Crone Koniferus. All around the edges of the chamber were dozens of tunnel entrances.

'Which way do you think we should go?' whispered Isabella.

'Let's go through that archway over there, with the two horrible-looking monsters carved all around it. I don't think we should go down another tunnel,' said Francesca, 'and besides, we don't know how long the batteries in our torches will last.'

As the girls walked silently across the sandy floor of the Great Cavern, towards and under the carved archway, Francesca and Isabella did not know the danger they were in, the monsters of the archway were actually live Venomous Viprads.

The only time they moved was when they had to eat. Their long arms disappeared into the sand, but should anything walk through the archway, each hand, which had six fingers and two

thumbs, would come out of the sand at lightning speed, grasp their prey, and gobble it down in just a few seconds.

As Francesca and Isabella walked nearer to the archway, the Venomous Viprads watched their every move, but never having seen humans before, who might be very dangerous enemies indeed, the Venomous Viprads decided not to attack them in case the weapons each one was carrying in their hand would burn them. Venomous Viprads do not like anything that is hot.

The girls walked safely through the archway and entered into another chamber.

In this chamber they saw hundreds and hundreds of very small moving sacks piled high. In each sack was a live wriggling snake. This was the food of the evil Koniferus.

Hanging down from the roof of the cavern, in nets made from webs spun by the many hundreds of spiders, were creatures that had three legs and five glaring purple eyes on the top of their bodies. These were called Spops, and they were the food of the Nibby Nabbies. The Nibby Nabbies eat only six meals a year in Inside World time.

This was the food cavern of the evil Koniferus and the Nibby Nabbies.

Along one side of the cavern wall were five openings, each one guarded by two Nibby Nabbies to protect the food from being stolen by their enemies.

When they saw the two girls, having never seen humans before, the terrified Nibby Nabbies panicked and ran off through the Viprad archway.

'Look over there,' said Francesca to Isabella, pointing towards the fleeing Nibby Nabbies. 'What strange creatures they are!'

Taking the Venomous Viprads by surprise, nine of the Nibby Nabbies escaped through the archway, but the one remaining Nibby Nabby was afraid that if he ran through the Viprad archway he would be gobbled up.

'Stay where you are!' shouted Francesca to the Nibby Nabby. 'Don't you dare run away.'

Nibby Nabbies always do as they are ordered to do.

'Come on,' said Isabella, 'let's go over and have a closer look at this strange creature.'

As the girls approached, the terrified Nibby Nabby placed one hand across his eyes.

Nibby Nabbies are not allowed to speak or take their hands from their eyes without permission.

'Do you understand what I am saying to you?' said Francesca.

The Nibby Nabby guard nodded his head.

'Take your hand away from your eyes and tell us who you are, and what this place is that we are in,' said Isabella.

'You are deep down in the Inside World, and I belong to one of the many tribes of Nibby Nabbies that live down here. I am Nibby Nabby 44.'

'Do you know the way back to the Outside World?' asked Francesca.

'No, I have never been to the Outside World,' he said, 'but I have heard Nibby Nabbies talk of a secret tunnel that is used by the Sleepless One when she returns there.'

'Who is the Sleepless One?' asked Isabella.

'She is a witch, and her name is Koniferus,' said the Nibby Nabby guard.

'Can you show us the way to this tunnel that leads to the Outside World?' asked Francesca.

'I think it's that way,' he said, pointing to one of the five openings in the wall that he had been guarding.

'Right,' said Francesca, 'let's get going.' Picking up a trident each, they set off.

'I must warn you,' said the Nibby Nabby, 'each of those openings lead into caverns where monsters live.'

'Which one should we go through?' asked Isabella.

'I do not know,' said the Nibby Nabby guard, 'I have never been into those caverns.'

'Right, that settles it, we shall go into the middle cavern,' said Francesca.

'That's where Klopolk lives,' said the Nibby Nabby.

'What sort of a creature is that?' asked Francesca.

'It has a large head, and a long body with four legs, and a long tail which also has four legs,' said the Nibby Nabby.

'How do you know, if you have never been into that cavern?' asked Francesca.

'I have seen Klopolk when standing guard. Sometimes Nibby Nabbies have thrown the creature some of our Spops for him to eat; the Spops make Klopolk very tired, and he soon goes to sleep,' said the Nibby Nabby.

'That's what we shall do then,' said Francesca, 'we shall gather lots of these Spops and feed them to that creature Klopolk.'

As the girls and the Nibby Nabby got closer to the entrance of Klopolk's cavern, Francesca asked Number 44 why the creature had never been into the food cavern.

'He is too big and fat, that's why we keep feeding him our Spops,' said the Nibby Nabby.

Francesca and Isabella peered through the opening into the gloomy light of the cavern. The girls switched on their torches and shone the beams of light around the cavern.

Nibby Nabby Number 44 was now more frightened than ever, as he watched light coming from the fingers of the girls. He would have liked to run away, but didn't dare. Nibby Nabbies always follow the orders they are given.

At the far end of the cavern, Klopolk with his glaring orange eyes, could just make out the two shadows of Francesca and Isabella.

Thinking to himself that the Nibby Nabby had come to feed him, Klopolk ran across the sandy floor of the Great Cavern with great speed.

As Klopolk got closer and closer to the entrance of the cavern, Francesca shouted to Isabella, 'Quick, let's back away a bit, that horrible creature is charging at us!'

But when Klopolk saw the girls, he quickly came to a stop, having never seen humans from the Outside World before. He was very wary indeed, and with his huge tail swishing from side to side, he stood, wondering what his next move should be.

'Come on,' said Francesca, 'let's gather up lots of these Spops and throw them into the cavern.'

The ravenous Klopolk gobbled the Spops up, and after a short while Francesca, Isabella and Nibby Nabby Number 44 watched as Klopolk slowly sank down on to his knees, rolled over on to his side, let out a great roar, and fell asleep.

'Now is our chance to get through this cavern and escape,' said Isabella, 'but first we must collect plenty of Spops and take them with us.'

Entering the cavern where Klopolk lay asleep, Francesca, Isabella and Nibby Nabby Number 44 gazed around.

'Let's switch on our torches again,' said Francesca. 'We must find a way out of here.'

'Look over there,' said Isabella. 'Looks like there is only one way out of this cavern.'

As the girls and the Nibby Nabby guard walked silently past Klopolk, they saw many small ledges along the walls of the cavern, and on each ledge were nine precious sparkling stones. This was the treasure cavern of the evil witch Koniferus.

'Don't touch any of those,' said the Nibby Nabby. 'I have been told that the evil Koniferus has cast a spell on them.'

'Come on,' said Francesca, 'let's get out of this cavern.'

At that moment Klopolk awoke from his sleep, and with a great groan he rolled over and stood back up on to his feet. Looking around, he could just see Francesca, Isabella and the Nibby Nabby leaving his cavern.

I shall wait, he thought to himself. *There is only one way back for that Nibby Nabby, and when he returns I shall make a meal of him.*

'Look,' said Isabella, 'there is a fountain over there! Come on, I am so thirsty, I would like a drink of water.'

'How do I return to the food cavern?' asked the Nibby Nabby.

'That's easy,' said Francesca, 'just throw all these Spops we brought with us to the creature Klopolk, and when he falls asleep make a dash for it.'

Little did the girls realise how close they had come to being captured by the Nibby Nabbies. When Francesca and Isabella had entered the Inside World, they had left a trail of footprints in the sand.

Forty-three Nibby Nabby guards had followed these

footprints, but when they reached the cavern where Klopolk was just waking up from his sleep, they dared not go any further.

When Francesca and Isabella reached the fountain, they both cupped their hands together and held them under the cascading water to get a drink.

As each droplet touched their hands it turned into a precious sparkling stone.

'What are we going to do next?' asked Isabella.

'Look over there,' said Francesca. 'I can see five tunnels. One of those could be our escape from this place. Let's take one of these sparkling stones each and see which of those tunnels will lead us into the Outside World.'

As the girls approached the tunnels they could hear a great snoring noise coming down from the first tunnel.

'There must be a horrible beast that lives down there,' whispered Isabella, trembling slightly.

'Look over there,' said Francesca, pointing to some footprints in the sand, which lead into the middle tunnel, 'that could be our way out.'

As they reached the tunnel entrance, Francesca and Isabella could feel a soft breeze drifting into the cavern from the Outside World.

'Come on, Isabella,' said Francesca, 'let's run down this tunnel as quick as we can, and get back into the Outside World.'

Back in the Outside World, Francesca said, 'Let's get our breath back and then get away from this place; we should find our picnic hamper and go home.'

As the girls wandered home, eating the food from the hamper and drinking their juice, Francesca said to Isabella, 'We had better not tell anyone what has happened to us today; nobody would believe us.'

'I agree,' said Isabella, 'it will be our secret.'

When the girls arrived home, Francesca's mummy asked the girls if they had enjoyed their picnic.

'Yes, thanks, we have had a lovely time, it's been very exiting,' said Francesca.

'Thank goodness it did not rain and spoil your picnic!' said Francesca's mummy.

Part Two

The Girls Disappear

Deep, deep down in the Inside World, the leader of the Nibby Nabbies has summoned together all the tribes. The noise of their chatter echoed around the Great Chamber.

'*SILENCE!*' roared their leader, 'You will now listen to the wisdom of the Crone.'

The withered old Crone appeared on the platform. She was 500 years old and had never been to sleep. Some called her the Sleepless One, but her real name was Koniferus the Crone.

Her hair was a tangle of rats' tails, she was dressed in a tattered, torn old gown, and on her arm was a large old bag full of squirming snakes of all sizes. She would occasionally pick one out of the bag and bite off its head, swallow it, and then throw the wriggling snake's body into the crowd of Nibby Nabbies. The one who managed to grab the snake's body would run off to feed its children with it.

'Why are we gathered here?' shouted one of the Nibby Nabbies.

'*SILENCE!*' screeched Koniferus, 'how dare you speak without my permission! Guards, seize that insolent creature and feed him to the Giant Crab.'

The guard dragged the screaming Nibby Nabby away.

'Help me, help me!' he cried, but no one dare help him. If they did they knew that the Giant Crab would take a larger meal than usual that night.

All the Nibby Nabbies put a hand over their mouths to prevent any noise, and to save them from being thrown to the Giant Crab.

Koniferus glared down on the hundreds of Nibby Nabbies.

'Now, as you know, I have just returned from visiting the

Kingdom of Wickedness. While I was away, two human girls from the Outside World have been down here and have escaped, taking with them one of my most precious jewels. Whichever one of you is responsible for letting them steal from me and then escape will make a meal for the crab!' she shrieked.

She paused.

Not a sound could be heard.

All the Nibby Nabbies kept their heads bowed. They dared not lift up their heads, for if any of them did, it meant certain death.

She glowered at the great crowd.

'I have gathered you all here because my precious jewel must be found and returned to me, and the two human girls must be brought before me for punishment,' shouted the old Crone.

Not a sound, not a movement came from the Nibby Nabbies. They were extremely frightened.

Koniferus pulled a snake out of her bag and bit off its head; she threw the snake's body into the crowd, but nobody moved; they were terrified.

'You will all go to the Outside World,' she shrieked, 'and bring back the jewel and the human girls.'

Snap. Crack. Off came another snake's head.

'One of you Nibby Nabbies come forward and stand before me,' she shouted.

The bravest of the Nibby Nabbies shuffled forward and with his head bowed, stood before the old Crone.

'*SPEAK*!' she commanded.

'Thank you, Evil One, for letting me speak,' he said timidly. 'We have never been to the Outside World; we do not know what it is like or how to get there.'

'Stupid, stupid creatures,' roared Koniferus, 'do you not know anything? Do I have to do *everything*? Go and find Metzler the mighty wizard; he has been to the Outside World many times, he will tell you how to get there.'

Relieved to get away from the old Crone alive, the Nibby Nabby ran off to find Metzler.

He ran through the many dark passages of the Inside World until he finally reached the darkest of caves, which was the home of the wizard.

'Metzler, oh mighty wizard, where are you?' he shouted. 'Koniferus the old Crone demands to speak to you.'

The wizard was nowhere to be seen.

Then there was a rustle of feathers, and a voice from above.

'I am up here; I have changed myself into a vulture for today. Tell the Crone I will see her, but first I must eat,' and with that he flew down and gobbled up a fat, slimy Tixit.

'Ah, that was very tasty,' he said when he had devoured the poor creature. 'I am now ready to face the old Crone, once I have changed myself into my wizard form.'

He mumbled some magic words, and once again took on the form of Metzler the mighty wizard, the most powerful being of the Inside World.

While the Crone was glowering down at the hundreds of Nibby Nabbies, waiting for one false move that would give her a reason to feed the Giant Crab again, a very tall person appeared on the stone platform.

He had very long hair and a long beard, his eyes were as black as midnight and he wore a long flowing garment which concealed many, many pockets that were full of bottles containing magic potions and pills. This was Metzler the mighty wizard.

In one pocket lived a one-eyed lizard.

The wizard had removed the lizard's other eye so he could leave it in the Outside World to spy on anyone or anything he wanted to know about.

A few days ago the wizard had disguised himself as a squirrel and gone to the Outside World with the lizard's eye. As a squirrel he had climbed up a tree in the garden where the human girls lived, and placed the eye in a tall tree.

Metzler now looked at the old Crone. He was the only being that Koniferus feared. He had far more power and magic than the old Crone would ever possess.

Metzler looked at the Sleepless One and asked why she wanted to see him.

The old Crone, turning her evil gaze of hatred away from the Nibby Nabbies, said, 'O, Wise One, while I was away visiting the Kingdom of Wickedness, two human girls entered the Inside World and stole my most precious jewel. I want it returned to me, and I want the human girls punished.

'I seek your wisdom on how to retrieve my jewel from the Outside World, and I need you to tell the Nibby Nabbies how to get there.'

'Very well,' said the Wizard, 'I am prepared to use my magical powers to get the Nibby Nabbies to the Outside World, but it will be very dangerous.'

Metzler searched in one of his many pockets, he pulled out the one-eyed lizard and looked into its one remaining eye.

Reflected in the eye of the lizard, the Wizard could see what the other eye in the tree was watching. It really was a most clever way of keeping an eye on things he wanted to know about; it most certainly was one of his cleverest magical tricks by far.

Reflected in the lizard's eye, he could see the two human girls playing outside in the garden. They were having a tea party, and they were very happy because Isabella was sleeping overnight as a special treat.

Turning and facing the old Crone, Metzler said, 'I know of a creature, a Throg, and he lives very close to the human girl's house. He once disobeyed my orders, and as a punishment I ordered him to live in the Outside World and spy for me. He lives next to the house where the girl named Francesca lives.'

Metzler continued, 'I will now go into a deep trance and summon the Throg to attend me down here in the Inside World.'

Metzler, in his long, flowing, colourful cloak, began waving his arms about and muttering strange-sounding words, then he was still.

Not a sound or movement from the Nibby Nabbies, they were terrified, for they had witnessed many times how easy it was for the mighty Metzler to be displeased, and in a flash transformed himself into some ugly and horrible creature.

Metzler's gaze turned to the Sleepless One. He said, 'I am now in command of the Nibby Nabbies' journey to the Outside World.'

Just at that moment, the Throg appeared before Metzler and the old Crone. The Nibby Nabbies had rushed off to get ready.

'Welcome, Throg,' said the magician.

'Thank you,' said Throg, 'but why do you need my presence

down here in the Inside World, and where are all the tribes of Nibby Nabbies?'

'They have gone to prepare themselves for a journey into the Outside World,' said the wizard. 'You must guide them there, Throg, for you know where the human girls live.'

'I know the place very well,' said Throg, 'I have lived in the drain next to Francesca's house for a long, long time. We must set off on our journey immediately, we have many underground tunnels to get through, and we must get to the house in the dark of night when everyone is asleep.'

The Nibby Nabbies returned to the huge cavern armed with their spears and weapons.

'You will not fail in your task!' shrieked the old Crone. 'If you do not succeed I will feed your children to the crab.'

Metzler searched in one of his many pockets and he pulled out a small orange bottle.

'Take this,' he said to the leader of the Nibby Nabbies. 'It is a powerful magic powder. Sprinkle it on the girls; it will keep them asleep long enough for you to get them away from the Outside World and back to us here.'

'Heed my words,' hissed Koniferus, 'if you want to see your children alive, do not fail.'

'Goodbye,' shouted Throg. 'We are ready to go to the Outside World and capture the human girls.'

Throg set off on the long underground journey, followed by hundreds of Nibby Nabbies.

Through the dark forest they went, past the small beck with even more bones and skeletons of many poor unfortunate creatures who had dared to drink its waters; past the fountain of diamonds and precious stones, where the two girls had not been able to resist filling their pockets. Past the lake were an enormous crocodile was forever waiting to leap out and snatch some unsuspecting creature and swallow it up. It was out of luck tonight though, for the Nibby Nabbies kept well away from the edge of the lake. They had witnessed too many of their own tribe being eaten by the creature. It was indeed a very dangerous place.

They did not go as far as the two-headed snake. Instead,

Throg led them through a dark, damp, underground tunnel, which would lead them to the well.

As they approached the entrance to the well, Throg whispered, 'We are here. Now, I need the two strongest Nibbies to lift the heavy stone slab so we can climb out.'

Grisch and Grosch, the mighty twins, came forward. 'We are ready!' they said, and began pushing the great stone off the well.

It was midnight and very dark as one by one the Nibby Nabbies climbed out.

'We will wait here,' said Grisch and Grosch, 'ready to pull the great slab back over the well when you return.'

'Good idea,' said Throg. Pointing to the house, he said. 'Now, this is the home of Francesca the human girl, you must climb up the wall of the house and find an unlocked window to get in.'

The Nibby Nabbies laid down their spears and weapons and started climbing up the building.

Luckily for them, earlier that evening Francesca's mummy had been making up a spare bed for Isabella, who was staying the night with her friend. While she was up there a neighbour had knocked on the door downstairs and she had hurried down the stairs to open the door, but in her hurry hadn't locked the bedroom shutters properly.

The Nibby Nabbies reached the window and carefully pushed the shutters to see if they would open. With a loud creak the shutters opened. The Nibby Nabbies waited in total silence, afraid that the human girls might wake up, but the girls slept on, and very quietly the Nibby Nabbies climbed into the girls' bedroom.

All was very quiet in the humans' house.

'Right,' whispered the leader of the Nibby Nabbies, as they surrounded the human girls' beds. 'Take the stopper out of the bottle and sprinkle the magic powder onto the girls. The dust will keep them asleep until we have delivered them to the Evil One.'

A big, black, hairy spider crawled out of bottle-top, and slowly the magic dust came out of the bottle.

'Has anyone found the jewel?' whispered Throg.

'I have found a box,' said one of the Nibby Nabbies. 'It is full of all sorts of jewels and I do not know which belongs to the old Crone.'

'Take them all,' said Throg. 'We must make certain we have the old Crone's jewel. Take them all to make sure we have the right one.'

Carefully, the Nibby Nabbies lifted the human girls out of their beds and carried them across to the open window, where many pairs of hands were waiting to lift them down to the ground.

With great speed they carried them to the well, and lowered them down into the innermost depths.

When all the Nibby Nabbies had assembled and been counted to make sure no one was left behind for the humans to find, the mighty twins pulled the great stone slab back over the well, and not a trace or sign of them ever having been there could be found.

Or so they thought…

Part Three
Escape

Quickly and silently, the hundreds of Nibby Nabbies followed Throg until they came to a huge cavern. In it was a great lake, and on the shores of the lake were thousands of bones and skulls.

Throg halted the marching Nibby Nabbies and whispered, 'Do not make a sound. Zenom lives in this great lake, and he will devour anything that dares to disturb him. Nibby Nabbies are his favourite meal; all the bones you see around you are the remains of hundreds of Nibby Nabbies.'

'What does Zenom look like?' whispered one of the Nibby Nabbies.

'I am the only one who knows,' said Throg. 'Zenom would not eat me, my skin is very poisonous, but nobody else who has ever disturbed Zenom has ever survived to tell the tale; Zenom has devoured them.

'He has four heads,' continued Throg, 'and he can gobble down four Nibby Nabbies in a flash.

'You must all be very quiet, not the tiniest sound from anyone,' whispered Throg. 'Pass the word down to all the Nibby Nabbies behind you – not a sound, otherwise death awaits. He can strike out of the lake at great speed.

'Now,' whispered Throg, 'we all have to cross the great lake. Over there is a shallow part, we shall have to wade across it without making a sound or splash.'

'But Nibby Nabbies cannot swim, and we hate getting wet,' said the leader of the Nibby Nabbies, 'we will have to go back.'

'Nonsense,' said Throg. 'Just for once you must overcome your fear of water and wade through the shallow part of the lake up you get to the waterfall cascading down into the lake. Behi waterfall is a tunnel which will lead us back into safety.

'Before we set off,' whispered Throg, 'make sure the human girls stay asleep, sprinkle some more magic dust over them; if they wake up and disturb Zenom you will all perish.'

The Nibby Nabbies, on their tiptoes, for they detested even the shallowest water, continued on their journey to the waterfall and the tunnel that would lead them back to the Great Cavern to deliver the human girls to Koniferus the Crone. It looked as though they had managed to escape Zenom's clutches, but right at the last moment, one of the Nibby Nabbies sneezed. Quick as lightning the four heads of Zenom appeared, but he only managed to snatch three of them, the others were all safely behind the waterfall.

Zenom sank back down into the murky depths of the lake to feast on the three unfortunate Nibby Nabbies.

Behind the waterfall was a long, dark, damp tunnel. The tunnel roof above the Nibby Nabbies' heads was a tangled mass of moss-covered branches and twigs.

Thankful to have escaped the clutches of Zenom, the remaining Nibby Nabbies marched on to deliver the two human girls to the old Crone Koniferus.

For all that the Nibby Nabbies were extremely quiet as they were marching down the tunnel, they had not escaped the attention of Porik, the silent predator, who was lurking above their heads and peering down at them.

Ah, thought Porik, *dinner has arrived at long last; my family will eat well tonight and for many days to come.*

With his legs pressed firmly to each side of the tunnel, Porik waited with patience until the exact moment arrived for him to strike down through a gap between the branches and twigs.

At last the moment arrived, and with a flash of speed that was quicker than the eye could see, down came Porik's proboscis, grasping the wriggling Nibby Nabby by the head as he hoisted it up to the roof of the tunnel and quickly gobbled it up.

Now, thought Porik, *it is time to feed my offspring, and also put some more of these creatures into my food store for later when food is scarce.*

Very quickly, Porik settled to work, silently hoisting up one

Nibby Nabby after another into the secret space between the branches and twigs, pushing the Nibby Nabbies into storage spaces in the sides of the wall and then sealing up the openings.

Good, good, thought Porik, *I now have a large secret larder of food.*

Luckily for the two humans, as they were being carried through the tunnel, Porik was too busy hiding his new food supply in the many secret places to notice them, and they escaped his clutches.

Or perhaps they were not so lucky, for the girls were getting closer and closer to being delivered to the Evil One.

Guided by Throg, on and on marched the silent Nibby Nabbies, carrying with them the two sleeping girls.

They approached the entrance to the Great Cavern and faced their most feared ordeal of the entire journey: they had to assemble themselves in front of the evil, Sleepless One.

When all the Nibby Nabbies were quietly standing in line, the old Crone glared down at them and screeched, 'I can see that you have carried out my orders and captured and returned the human girls to the Inside World. I will think of a suitable punishment for these insolent human girls when they awaken from their slumber. In the meantime, my trusty guards will ensure they are escorted and taken away to the high dungeon which is guarded by the hovering Death Bug, the most poisonous creature in the Inside World. One touch from its sharp claws means instant death.'

'*TAKE THEM AWAY, GUARDS*!' screamed Koniferus.

When the guards had carried the human girls away to the high dungeon, she turned her evil gaze on to the hundreds of silent Nibby Nabbies.

'I see that some of you are missing.' the Evil One said. 'Where are they? If any of them have been left on the Outside World to be captured by humans, I will punish whoever is responsible for not counting them properly as they entered the well to return to the Inside World.

'I order the chief Nibby Nabby to come forward to answer my questions.'

The leader of the Nibby Nabbies scuttled forward and stood before the Crone.

'I ordered you to bring the human girls down to me, and you

have done so, but where is my precious jewel? You have my permission to speak,' she said.

'Thank you, Evil One,' the leader of the Nibby Nabbies began timidly. 'When we entered the human girls' bedroom and captured them, we saw a box of shiny trinkets on a table, but not knowing which belonged to you, we brought the whole box of jewels for you to claim which is yours.'

'Very well,' continued Koniferus. 'Give me the box and I will find my jewel. As I asked earlier, why are some members of your tribe missing? Explain to me where they are.'

'O, Great One,' said the leader, 'on leaving the Inside World to capture the human girls the tribe has been through a terrible ordeal.

'The brave and gallant Throg guided us to the Outside World through many, many tunnels, and at last we reached the bottom of the well, which is next to the human girl's house. It has been unused for many years, and no water has been in it for a long time.

'On our return journey to the Inside World,' continued the leader, 'we were attacked by evil monsters, who were so cunning, quick and silent, we did not even see them as they swooped down, caught and gobbled up some of our tribe.'

'I am aware of these monsters,' hissed Koniferus. 'If some of your tribe are so slow and stupid that they get themselves caught, then they deserved to be devoured. Now, tell me how many of your tribe are missing. We must make certain no one has been left in the Outside World to be found and questioned about our Inside World.'

'Forty-one are missing,' said the leader of the Nibby Nabbies; 'forty-one of our tribe have perished in order to obey your command to capture the human girls and retrieve your precious jewel.'

'Where is Metzler?' shouted the old Crone. 'Go find him, we must ask him to look into the lizard's eye to make sure that nobody was left behind in the Outside World.'

Metzler was not far away. He had been watching the arrival of the two human girls and the return of the Nibby Nabbies.

The Nibby Nabby who had been ordered by Koniferus to find

Metzler soon found him, and in a timid, quiet voice said, 'O, Mighty One, the old Crone requests your presence, she wishes you to peer into the lizard's eye to make certain that nobody has been left behind in the Outside World.'

'Very well,' said Metzler. 'Go tell the old Crone I will be there shortly, as soon as I have finished this little experiment.'

The Nibby Nabby, relieved to have got away from the wizard safely, ran off quickly to pass on the message to the old Crone.

When Metzler finally arrived in the Great Cavern, the old Crone screeched 'O, mighty Metzler, thank you for appearing so promptly. There are forty-one Nibby Nabbies missing, please be kind enough to look in the lizard's eye and see if any of them have been left behind in the Outside World. If anyone or anything has been left I will punish the whole tribe severely.'

Metzler took the one-eyed lizard out of one of his many pockets. He looked in the lizard's eye; he could see the well, and beside the well he could see a weapon, with Nibby Nabby Number 44 written on it. That was all he saw.

Oh dear, he thought, *someone is going to be in trouble when the old Crone finds out.*

Metzler turned to Koniferus. 'I see nothing unusual on the Outside World, the humans are still asleep, and everything is as it should be; there are no signs that anyone has been there or been left behind from the Inside World.'

'Thank you, Mighty One,' croaked Koniferus. 'For once the Nibby Nabbies have carried out my orders successfully and no one will have to be punished. I will now go to the high dungeon and see if the human girls have woken up.'

On the same night that Francesca and Isabella had been kidnapped, strange things were happening on the Outside World.

Someone had indeed been left behind from the Inside World, and it was Nibby Nabby Number 44. He could not lift the heavy stone slab covering the well to return to the Inside World. He then remembered there was another way into the Inside World, which was down on Femur beach.

Making his way quietly down to the beach, and standing on the sea shore, he could hear sounds of muffled voices and the

splashing of oars coming from the sea – he could just make out some rowing boats approaching the beach. Fearing for his life he ran and hid behind a rock.

Out of the misty darkness, lit only by a single moonbeam, seven rowing boats landed on the beach.

With barely a sound, seventy pirates climbed out of the boats with their swords and cutlasses gleaming in the faint moonlight. Their leader was the fearsome, cut-throat Blackbeard,

'Gather round me, men,' said Blackbeard. 'We are very close to the house where the young girl lives whose granddad stole our treasure, sunk our boat and had us locked up and then taken to Shark Island. We will finally get our revenge! We will kidnap the girl and demand a very large ransom for her safe return.'

Nibby Nabby 44 was behind the rock listening to every word being spoken. A spider crab scuttled over his toes and made him jump.

'What's that noise?' shouted Scarface, as he ran to the rock from where the noise had come. The Nibby Nabby tried to hide but Scarface had seen him, picked him up by the scruff of his neck and threw him down to land in front of Blackbeard.

'What a strange looking creature,' said Blackbeard. 'Who are you and where do you come from? Speak and tell me the truth,' he shouted, brandishing his cutlass.

'I live down in the Inside World,' said the terrified Nibby Nabby. 'My tribe came to the Outside World to capture two human girls and take them back to the old Crone Koniferus, for them to be punished for stealing her most precious jewel.'

'*JEWEL*? shouted Blackbeard, 'tell me all about this jewel, and who is Koniferus? And where is this Inside World you come from?'

The terrified Nibby Nabby described the Inside World and all about the evil Crone Koniferus, Metzler the mighty wizard, Throg, the capture of the two human girls, Zenom the four-headed monster, Porik the silent predator, the hovering Death Bug, the high dungeon and most importantly – the magic cascading fountain.

'The entrance to the Inside World is through that cave across the beach, under the rocks,' explained the trembling Nibby

Nabby. 'But I warn you, the entrance to the Inside World is guarded by a Giant Crab. Only two human people have ever managed to get past the crab and into the Inside World.'

'Right,' said Blackbeard, 'you will show me the way to the Giant Crab. But first, some of you men go and bring some lanterns from the boats. The rest of you follow me, it will be your task to sneak up on the crab and tie his pincer claws together.'

The pirates, with Nibby Nabby 44 leading, made their way very silently to the entrance of the dark and eerie cave.

'Gather around me, you motley lot of vagabonds, and heed my words,' whispered Blackbeard. 'Fourteen men are to follow Dreadlocks, whom I have put in charge of overpowering the Giant Crab. When this is done, signal to me and I will lead the men down to the cave.'

A short time later, peering through the darkness, Blackbeard could just make out a small light swinging to and fro.

'Right men, that's the signal. Follow me.'

Barely making a sound, the pirates made their way down through the tunnel of the cave, and before long they met up with their comrades.

Meanwhile, in the high dungeon, Francesca and Isabella were just waking up.

When they looked around them they were very frightened. 'Where are we?' asked Isabella.

'I don't know,' said Francesca, 'but let's try not to be afraid. Something or somebody must have kidnapped us during the night. This looks very much like a dungeon to me.'

'But if this is a dungeon, why does it not have a locked door keeping us in?'

'I don't know,' replied Francesca, 'but whatever it is, it means we can make our escape through that open doorway over there.'

Holding hands, the girls went to leave the dungeon, but just as they reached the doorway, down from the dark roof space dropped the evil, hovering Death Bug. His job was to make sure the girls did not escape.

Screaming in fright, Francesca and Isabella ran back into the dungeon.

'What a dreadful creature that is!' said Izzy. 'How on earth are we going to escape from this awful place now?'

'Don't worry, we will think of something to get ourselves out of here,' said Francesca.

But the hovering Death Bug had different ideas. He was waiting for the girls to go near the entrance again, if they did, he would be ready to gobble them up.

Just at that moment the girls heard a shrill voice asking them if they were awake.

'Yes we are, but who are you, can you help us to escape from this place? There is a terrible creature hovering in the doorway, which is waiting to catch us if we try and escape,' shouted Francesca.

'I am Koniferus, the Sleepless One; do not try to get past the hovering Death Bug.'

Back in the tunnel, from the glow of their lanterns, the pirates gazed upon the huge crab with its pincer claws bound together, and two angry eyes glaring at its capturers.

'Well done, Dreadlocks,' said Blackbeard, 'I knew I could rely on you. That will keep the crab from moving about for some time.'

'Now,' said Blackbeard to Nibby Nabby 44, 'show us the way in to your Inside World.'

'Very well,' said the Nibby Nabby. 'But I warn you all, once you have entered the Inside World from here, you cannot return to your Outside World by this way; the entrance disappears once you have walked through it.'

'Never mind that,' said Blackbeard. 'Just lead the way, me and this bunch of villains will do the rest.'

Quietly each of them stepped through the tunnel.

'There's no going back now, men,' said Blackbeard. 'Let's get going. Show us the way to the fountain of precious stones, Nibby Nabby.'

Back in the Great Chamber, peering up, Koniferus could see the hovering Death Bug swinging to and fro at the entrance to the high dungeon. Speaking to her guards, the Crone ordered them to climb the steps to the high dungeon and bring down the human girls.

Fearing for their lives, one of the guards signalled to the Evil One that he wished to speak to her.

The Crone looked at the Nibby Nabby guard.

'Very well,' she screeched at him. 'Speak, what have you to say?'

'O, Great One,' said the guard. 'If we climb the steps up to the high dungeon and are touched by the poisonous Death Bug, we will die, and you will be left without any guards.'

'*SILENCE*,' the Crone shouted at the Nibby Nabby, glaring down at him with her evil eyes, 'Do you think I do not know that?'

Lifting her head up to the hovering Death Bug, she cried, 'Be gone into the darkness of the roof, and do not return until the girls have been taken away.'

On hearing this order from the Crone, the Death Bug ran up its web and hid in the darkness of the roof, and there it waited for an opportunity to feed itself.

'The Death Bug has gone. Six of you guards climb up the stairs and bring the human girls down to me; the remaining four guards will stay with me,' ordered the old Crone.

When the Nibby Nabby guards reached the entrance to the ill-lit dungeon, they could just see Francesca and Isabella in the gloom. 'You human girls are to follow us,' they told them.

'Have you come to rescue us?' asked Francesca.

'Silence!' said the guard. 'We have been ordered not to answer any of your questions. You will follow us down the steps, and no tricks from either of you. Three guards will go first, then you two, followed by three guards at the rear.'

Just as the last Nibby Nabby was on the top step, ready to make his way down, from out of the darkness and with lightning speed, the Death Bug swooped down, grabbed the Nibby Nabby, and pulled himself back into the roof space, before settling down to enjoy his supper.

When Francesca and Isabella, escorted by the remaining guards, reached the bottom of the steps, Koniferus the evil witch was glaring down on the human girls.

Rubbing her gnarled and crooked hands together, the evil one screeched, 'You human girls will follow me into the Great Chamber. It will be there that I decide on the punishment you deserve for daring to enter the Inside World, and for stealing my most precious jewel.'

The old Crone slowly shuffled away, followed by Francesca and Isabella, escorted by the Nibby Nabby guards.

Meanwhile, the pirates, guided by Nibby Nabby 44, were approaching the Great Chamber.

Even before they arrived there, a high raucous voice could be heard echoing down the tunnel.

'What is that and where is it coming from?' whispered Blackbeard to the Nibby Nabby.

'It is Koniferus, the evil one, she must have all the Nibby Nabby tribes in front of her.'

Speaking quietly to Dreadlocks, Blackbeard told him to pass the word back to the rest of the pirates to stay where they were, while he and Nibby Nabby 44 crept forward quietly to see what was awaiting them.

They hid behind a huge stone slab at the entrance to the huge chamber, and saw Francesca and Isabella standing in front of the evil old witch.

'Those are the two human girls we were ordered to capture and bring back to the old Crone,' whispered Nibby Nabby.

Yes thought Blackbeard, *those are the girls I have come to capture and hold for a large ransom. If things go according to plan, not only will I have sacks full of precious stones, but also ransom money to boot.*

'Where is the cascading fountain?' whispered Blackbeard to the Nibby Nabby.

'It is across the Great Chamber, through that archway behind the old crone, but I warn you, since those human girls went away with the Crone's precious jewel, she now has it guarded by the fearsome Grogon.'

'What does this Grogon look like?' asked Blackbeard.

'It is a huge two-headed monster with thick scales to protect its body; even your swords and cutlasses will not penetrate those scales.'

'There will be other ways to deal with Grogon,' said Blackbeard. 'In the meantime, I want to rescue those girls, but first let us listen to what the old Crone is saying to them.'

The old Crone was thinking about how to punish the girls.

Pointing a long, twisted finger at them, she cackled, 'You will be taken back to the high dungeon and fed until you are both as fat as dumplings, and then you will be a tasty meal for Grogon.'

'Don't try and frighten us, you toothless, ugly old hell-hag,' shouted Francesca.

Just at that moment, Metzler appeared on the platform. 'O, Wise One' said the Crone, 'why are you here?'

'I have grave news,' said Metzler, 'there are seventy pirates from the Outside World down here. They intend to rescue the human girls and take away as many precious jewels as possible.'

'*WHAT*?' screamed the Crone. 'How did they get down here? Never mind that. Guards, take the human girls back to the high dungeon; the rest of you miserable Nibby Nabbies, prepare to defend me.'

'Come along with us,' the guards said to the girls, taking hold of their prisoners.

'How dare you touch us!' said Izzy, and with that she punched the guard on the nose.

'Well done, Izzy!' said Francesca. 'Oh, look, the Nibby Nabby has green blood coming from his nose.'

Seeing all this, Blackbeard summoned the rest of the pirates.

'It's time for battle, men,' he said. 'But first let me tell you, those girls must be rescued, they are worth a large ransom to us in the Outside World, and remember, swords and cutlasses must not be used, you can punch, kick, bite and scratch, but no one must be killed.'

Then with a great war cry, seventy pirates charged into the throng of hundreds of Nibby Nabbies.

On the platform, Francesca punched a Nibby Nabby guard in the eye.

'Ouch,' he shouted. 'I will have a black eye tomorrow morning.'

'In that case you may as well have two black eyes,' said Francesca, and punched him in the other eye.

'Come on, Izzy,' she shouted. 'Let's join in the fight, we will teach these Nibby Nabbies to kidnap us.'

Jumping off the platform, the girls flung themselves into the fight. For two hours the Great Chamber echoed to the sounds of screams and shouts as the two sides kicked, punched and bit their opponents, with Francesca and Isabella fighting side by side with the pirates. Slowly but surely the pirates and the girls were winning the battle. The old Crone, seeing the fight was being lost, scuttled away out of the Great Chamber, and down into her cellar where she lived.

A few moments later, a very loud voice boomed out over the sounds of fighting. '*I COMMAND YOU TO STOP THIS FIGHTING AT ONCE!*'

It was the mighty Metzler.

When both sides had stopped fighting, and the noise of the battle had faded away, all that could be heard were the moans and groans of the Nibby Nabbies and pirates alike, who had black eyes and broken noses as they lay on the floor of the Great Chamber, rolling about in pain.

'Are you all right, Isabella?' asked Francesca.

'I'm fine.'

'Me too,' said Francesca. 'Better still when I get my breath back.'

Looking up at the platform to see who had ordered them to stop fighting, they saw for the first time Metzler the Wise One.

'I wonder who he is,' whispered Isabella.

'I don't know,' replied Francesca 'but I hope he is not evil like that horrible witch.'

'I want twenty able-bodied Nibby Nabbies to follow the evil one down to the cellar where she lives and stand guard outside the entrance, and make sure you lock the door,' said Metzler.

'But we have never been down to where the Crone lives,' said one of the timid Nibby Nabbies, 'and besides, you know what terrible things she can do to us.'

'Have no fear,' said Metzler. 'No harm will come to you, now go and carry out my orders.'

Quickly, the Nibby Nabbies ran off to obey Metzler's orders.

Turning his gaze down onto the floor of the Great Chamber, 'Which one of you Outside people is the leader?' asked Metzler.

'I am,' said Blackbeard, as he pulled a Nibby Nabby off his back who was trying to bite his ear off.

'What are you doing in our Inside World?' asked Metzler. 'Only two humans have ever been down here before but they escaped. Now they have been brought back to be punished by the old Crone; I am talking about the girls who have been fighting at your side. What is your name, pirate leader?'

'My name is Blackbeard.'

'Very well, Blackbeard,' said Metzler. 'Tell me why you and your men have come down into this World.'

'We have heard of a cascading fountain, whose water turns to precious stones when humans put their hands under the droplets,' said Blackbeard. 'We want to fill our sacks with jewels and take them back to the Outside World. We will be very rich.'

'I see,' said Metzler. 'And what about those two girls?'

'Ah,' said Blackbeard. 'We will take them back with us, but before I return them to their parents, I will want my treasure back, it was stolen from me by that girl's grandparent,' pointing a finger at Francesca.

'You have forgotten one or two very important things,' said Metzler.

'What are those?' asked Blackbeard.

'Firstly, you will have to fight the Grogon if you want to take the precious jewels to the Outside World.'

'We are willing to fight this creature, aren't we lads?' said Blackbeard.

'Aye, Aye!' shouted the seventy pirates, waving their cutlasses and swords in the air.

'What else?' said Blackbeard to Metzler.

'You have to find your way out of the Inside World, and I am the only one who knows the way out,' said Metzler, 'but if you defeat Grogon and drive him away from the fountain so the Nibby Nabbies can have a drink of water, I will allow you to leave. They are very thirsty, and have not had a drink since the evil Crone ordered Grogon to guard the fountain. Only Nibby Nabbies can drink this water without it turning to precious stones!'

'Who is going to show me where this fountain is?' asked Blackbeard.

'It will be the same Nibby Nabby that showed you the way in,' said Metzler.

'Where has he got to, I wonder,' said Blackbeard.

'Come out from behind that rock, Number 44,' ordered Metzler.

The frightened Nibby Nabby hurried across the Great Chamber, and stood in front of Metzler and Blackbeard. 'Why were you hiding?' asked Metzler.

'O, Wise One, I was afraid of what the evil Crone would have done to me for showing these humans the way into the Inside World.'

While all this talking was going on, Francesca and Isabella were whispering to one another about how they would escape from the pirates once they were back in the Outside World.

'Well, I think our best chance would be to simply run away,' said Francesca. 'Don't forget, they will have heavy sacks and pockets full of precious stones, they won't be able to run as fast as us.'

'Good idea,' said Isabella, 'that's our plan then. All we need to do now is be patient.'

'Now,' said Metzler to Nibby Nabby 44, 'you will guide these pirates to the Grogon and stay with them until it has been slain or driven away. When this is done, you will return here and report to me.'

'I will obey, O, Wise One,' said the Nibby Nabby.

'Just one moment,' said Blackbeard. 'When I have beaten this Grogon, how will I know which way to lead my men and these girls out of this Inside World?'

'When I hear that you have beaten the Grogon, I will send Number 44 back to show you the way out.'

'Very well,' said Blackbeard. 'I will accept your word, but if there is any treachery from you, I will return with my men and I will take my revenge on all of you.'

'Let's get started,' said Blackbeard. 'We have not got much time left, I want all of us to be aboard ship and back at sea before sunrise.

'Right,' said Blackbeard to Nibby Nabby 44. 'Show us the way to Grogon.'

The pirates and the girls followed Nibby Nabby 44 through many winding tunnels. 'Stop!' said Blackbeard to his men. 'Listen, I can hear cascading water, we cannot be far away from the Grogon and the fountain. Have your cutlasses and swords at the ready, men; if we don't defeat this creature, we will never leave with our treasures and escape to the Outside World.'

Quietly the Nibby Nabby, the pirates and Francesca and Isabella made their way to where the sound of cascading water was coming from.

'This is as far as I go,' said the Nibby Nabby. 'Over there is the entrance to a large cave, inside you will find the fountain and the Grogon; I will wait here until you have beaten it.'

'You girls stay here with the Nibby Nabby,' said the pirate leader. 'Come on, men,' said Blackbeard. 'We have no time to lose.'

The seventy pirates and their leader entered the cave. Standing next to the fountain they saw the two-headed monster, Grogon.

'I have never seen anything like that in all my life,' said Blackbeard.

The Grogon had never seen humans from the Outside World either, and if they tasted as bad as they smelled, it would certainly not wish to eat one, it thought.

'Right men, if we are going to make ourselves very rich, we have to get rid of this beast one way or another.'

'Let's just rush him,' said Dreadlocks. 'There are seventy of us, we will overpower him and tie him up.'

'You're right,' said Blackbeard, 'form a half-circle around the beast, and when I give the order, charge.'

While the pirates were taking up their positions, Blackbeard ordered one of the pirates to sneak round the back of the fountain and put his hands under the cascading water to make sure the droplets did indeed turn into precious stones. He did not wish to have a fight if the story was untrue.

A few moments later the pirate shouted out, 'It's true Captain, it's true, the water has turned into precious jewels.'

'That's what we have come here for, men,' and with a great bellow shouted, '*CHARGE!*'

When the girls heard this battle cry echo round the cave, Francesca said to her friend, 'Let's go the entrance of the cave and watch the fight, I want to see what this monster looks like.'

The girls arrived just as the pirates charged at the snarling Grogon. 'What a fearsome looking creature he is,' said Francesca.

The first eight pirates who hurled themselves onto the Grogon were flung away to the far sides of the cave.

'Keep going, men!' bellowed Blackbeard above the uproar of the fight, 'and get ready with those ropes.'

More and more pirates grappled with the Grogon; the fight lasted a full hour but then the Grogon's strength gave way and the exhausted monster was quickly tied up.

'Well done, men,' shouted Blackbeard, 'we have won!' A great cheer rose up from the pirates.

Seeing the girls at the entrance to the cave, Blackbeard shouted, 'You girls go and tell that Nibby Nabby he must inform the wizard that the Grogon has been defeated, and then to get back here as quickly as possible to show us the way out, then you girls come back here.'

'Right,' shouted the girls, and hurried off.

'Come on, men, get these bags filled up with the jewels, and don't forget to fill your pockets as well.'

All the pirates gathered round the fountain holding out their greedy hands, and as the droplets of water turned into jewels, they started filling their sacks and pockets.

'Can we help?' asked Francesca.

'OK,' said Blackbeard, 'but don't get in the way, these pirates are a rough lot.'

'We won't,' said Isabella.

'Right,' whispered Francesca, 'let's get as many precious stones into the pockets of these pirates as we can; it will slow them down for when we make our escape.'

In the Great Cavern, Nibby Nabby 44 stood in front of Metzler. 'O, Wise One,' he said, 'the humans have defeated the Grogon, and they are waiting for me to show them the way to the Outside World.'

'Very well,' said Metzler. 'You may return to the cascading fountain, but only when the pirate leader agrees to let the human girls go free, I will allow you to guide them to their Outside World. You will lead them to the back of the cave and there you will see five openings. Tell the pirates to follow you through the middle one. Now go and carry out my orders. If you survive, I will make you Chief Nibby Nabby.'

The Nibby Nabby ran back to the cave of the cascading fountain and told the pirate leader what Metzler had said. Blackbeard agreed to let the girls go free once they returned to the Outside World.

'The girls must be the first to follow me,' said Number 44, 'they will be the first to leave the Inside World and return to the Outside World. They can make sure the coast is clear for the rest of you to leave.'

'That's OK by me,' said Blackbeard. 'Now, which way do we go?'

'Follow me,' said the Nibby Nabby, as he led them towards the five tunnels.

The pirates lifted their heavy bags of precious stones onto their shoulders and off they went.

'Stop here, men,' said Blackbeard. 'Before we go through the middle tunnel, two of you go and have a look, just to make sure this is not a trap.'

'But what about our jewels?' asked the two pirates.

'You can leave them here, nobody will touch them,' said Blackbeard.

When the pirates had left, Francesca and Isabella sat down on a large rock.

'Do you think Blackbeard will keep his word and let us go once we reach the Outside World?' asked Isabella.

'I don't trust him one bit,' replied Francesca.

Blackbeard was having the same thoughts… *Once we are out of here and safely back in the Outside World, out of Metzler's reach, I will hold the girls for ransom.*

When the two pirates returned, they said that they could not see any danger, but that the middle tunnel was very narrow and steep.

'It will be, you idiots, we are a long way down here,' shouted Blackbeard, 'let's get going.'

As they reached the entrance to the middle tunnel, Nibby Nabby 44 said, 'I have to return now and report back to Metzler, I will tell him I have carried out his commands but don't forget, the human girls must go first, or Metzler's magic will keep you down here in the Inside World for ever.'

'Right,' said Blackbeard, 'you two girls lead on, we will follow.'

Quickly, Francesca and Isabella ran up the steep slope of the tunnel. 'Slow down,' shouted Blackbeard to the girls, 'you are getting too far in front of us.'

The greedy pirates carrying and dragging the heavy sacks of jewels were left behind on reaching the top-most part of the tunnel.

Francesca and Isabella came to a dead end.

'What do we do now?' asked Isabella.

'I don't know,' said Francesca, 'but I can hear the pirates getting closer.'

Looking up to see if there was another way of escape to the Outside World, Francesca could see a huge head with three glaring red eyes, and a very long, yellow, hooked beak looking down on the girls. This was Kroth, the keeper to the Outside World cavern. Its long great wings hung down and touched the ground of the cave.

Very slowly, the wings opened to let Francesca and Isabella escape to the Outside World. On hearing the moans and groans of the pirates carrying their heavy sacks of jewels, getting closer and closer, Isabella shouted, 'Come on, let's get out of here!'

The girls ran through the opening and into the darkness of the night, onto a beach. Looking over their shoulders to see if they were being followed, they could see nothing; the exit had disappeared.

'Come on,' said Francesca. 'Let's run home as fast as we can.'

From behind them, out of the darkness, they heard Dreadlocks shout out, 'Where are the girls?'

'Never mind them,' said Blackbeard. 'Get the boats loaded up and we will be gone, I want to be well out to sea before dawn, there will be another day to come back for them.'

Francesca and Isabella were hiding behind some large rocks.

Suddenly a great bolt of lightning lit up the dark sky, and they could just make out the pirates' boats disappearing into the night.

'Hooray, the dreadful pirates have gone,' said Isabella.

When the two girls had made their way to Francesca's home, they stood outside the front door. 'Oh dear,' said Isabella, 'how are we going to get in, we cannot climb up to the bedroom window, it is too high.'

At that moment, the door opened silently.

'I wonder how that happened?' whispered Francesca. 'Come on, let's go to bed, I am very tired.'

As the girls were climbing the stairs, the door closed quietly behind them and the key turned in the lock without a sound. Metzler's magic had done its work.

Just before Francesca and Isabella fell asleep in their beds, Francesca said, 'Well that has been a very exiting time for us, and all because of a precious jewel.'

'I have brought a few back with me,' said Izzy.

'So have I,' said Francesca, and with a little giggle both girls fell asleep.

In the cellar, deep down in the Inside World, and still being guarded by the Nibby Nabbies, Koniferus the Crone sat rocking forwards and backwards in her rocking chair.

She was thinking of a way to escape.

'I will escape,' she said to herself, 'and when I do, I will have my revenge on those two girls who are my sworn enemies.'

'*One day*,' she repeated to herself, screeching and cackling. '*One day…*'

Part Four

The Witches' Coven

At midnight, by the glow of a full moon, in a large clearing deep in Femur Forest, the Ancient Witch was preparing a stew of toads, lizards, frogs, spiders, rats, mice, earwigs and worms in a large black cauldron.

Very good, she thought to herself, *now I shall light the sticks under the cauldron, and by the time my sister witches arrive, this delicious supper should be ready for us to eat.*

Just as the stew was starting to simmer in the cauldron, the Ancient Witch began to hear faint noises coming out of the night sky.

'Ah, my sister witches are arriving for the Coven.'

As each of the twelve witches floated silently down to the forest clearing, they were greeted by the Ancient Witch.

'Welcome, Hexe and Gudrun.

'Welcome, Truckle and Trackle.

'Welcome, Pretzel and Strumpel.

'Welcome, Pumper and Nickel.

'Welcome, Wimple and Gogol.

'Welcome, Spottle and Herika.

'Welcome to the Coven, dear sisters. After we have recited the Witches' Code, and eaten this delicious meal, we shall plan how to rescue our sister Koniferus from deep down in the Inside World.

'Now, my sister witches, let us form a circle and hold our broomsticks aloft. We shall then recite our Historic Witches' Code.'

Gathering round, the witches held their broomsticks in the air, and with their heads bowed low, cackled the Witches' Code.

We swear by the warts on the end of our noses
And the pimples and spots on our chins
We promise to cast spells in large and small doses
And be true to the Coven we're in.
(And do lots of other nasty and evil things.)

'Well done, my sisters,' screeched the old Crone. 'Now we shall all eat this delicious broth I have prepared for you.'

The witches rushed to a pile of ladles that lay on the ground, pushing each other out of the way.

The first witch to get a ladle hurried back to the cauldron, it was Gudrun and she plunged her ladle into the broth and came out with a juicy fat toad.

'That's mine!' bellowed Hexe, 'I saw it first.'

'Well, it's too late now,' said Gudrun, as she opened her mouth and greedily chewed and swallowed the toad.

Meanwhile the other witches were busily pushing and shoving each other out of the way to get their ladles into the cauldron.

'Look what I have,' shouted Wimple, 'a lizard!'

She quickly scuttled off into the forest to eat it before one of the other witches could steal it from her.

When all the broth had been devoured, the Ancient witch said, 'did you enjoy your stew, dear sisters?'

'Yes, yes,' they replied.

'Well, I did not,' said Truckle, 'all I managed to get was an earwig and a spider's leg.'

'It was the most delicious broth I have ever eaten,' said Pumper, 'I loved the big fat juicy rat and the tasty worms.' Then she burped, 'Oh dear, I think I may have been too greedy and eaten too much.'

'Now that we have eaten,' said the Ancient Witch, 'I will whisper my plan to you my sisters, on how we will rescue our sister Koniferus.'

'There are two girls who live not very far away from here. Throg has told me they have been down into the Inside World twice, and have managed to escape both times.'

'What are their names?' asked Spottle.

'Keep your voice down,' said the Ancient One, 'we could be overheard. Their names are Francesca and Isabella.'

'Now this is my plan,' whispered the Ancient Witch.

'I know the house in which one of the girls live, Throg has told me; the girl's name is Francesca.'

'But, Ancient One, how are we going to make these girls, who are enemies of our sister Koniferus, guide us down into the Inside World?' asked Gudrun.

'We shall cast a magic spell on them, and then we shall have them in our power,' said the Ancient Witch.

All the Coven shrieked their delight at this plan.

'Now, sisters, our Witches' Coven is over for tonight. I want you all to return in four midnights' time to this very place. Now go before it is morning time.'

The witches climbed on their magic broomsticks, and were silently carried off into the night.

Down at the end of the cave to the Inside World, the Giant Crab had managed to free himself from the ropes that the pirates had tied his pincer claws together with.

He had not eaten any food for three nights, and was very hungry indeed.

I will devour anything or anybody that dares to enter my cave, he thought to himself.

Meanwhile, down in the Inside World, the Grogon had also managed to bite through the ropes the pirates had tied it up with.

On freeing itself, the huge monster let out a great roar that echoed all around the cavern.

It ran off to find the pirates and take its revenge on them, but to no avail, the pirates had gone.

Never mind, thought the Grogon. *Pirates are greedy for treasure, they will return, and when they do I will give them such a thrashing, that they will wish they had never returned down here to the Inside World for a second time.*

In the Outside World, Francesca and Izzy were planning to have a midnight feast on Femur beach.

'We will have to leave my house very quietly, when my parents are asleep,' said Francesca.

'When will that be?' asked Isabella.

'We will go in four nights' time,' said Francesca.

'I will ask my parents if I can stay with you that night,' said Isabella, 'and if they let me, I will bring some food for our midnight feast.'

The following day, when Francesca and Isabella met at school, Izzy told Francesca that her parents had agreed to let her stay overnight at her house.

'Oh, good,' said Francesca, 'now we shall have to plan what to take with us.'

After four midnights had passed, at the clearing in the forest, the Ancient Witch waited for the arrival of the Coven.

Very shortly she heard the familiar sound of the witches arriving as they gently floated down to the ground.

'Welcome, my sisters,' cackled the Ancient Witch, 'are you all here?'

Looking around, the Ancient Witch could only count eleven witches.

'Where is Gogol?' she screeched.

'I am up here stuck in this tree,' came a wail from above. 'I missed the clearing and crashed into this tree,' she said.

'That Gogol is an idiot,' said Herika. 'She has never learned to fly her broomstick properly. Only last week she missed her target and plunged into a lake.'

'One of you go and help the fool down,' cackled the Ancient Witch.

When this was done, and they were all assembled, the Ancient Witch said, 'Now, we have agreed on the plan to rescue our Sister Witch, I now want two volunteers who are willing to go into the Inside World and face all the dangers from the monsters down there.'

'Why do you want two of us?' asked Pretzel.

'I do not trust the girls. I have been told that they are very quick and clever. If they run off and leave you down in the Inside World, how would you find your way out? You would be captured by the Nibby Nabbies and held prisoner down in the Inside World. If there are two of you, it will be easier to keep your eyes on the girls, and make sure they do not get up to any trickery or mischief.

'Right,' continued the Ancient Witch. 'We do not have a minute to lose, who is going to volunteer?' she said, casting her glaring eyes over the Coven of witches.

'I will go,' said Hexe.

'Me too,' shouted Gudrun.

'Well done, my sisters,' said the Ancient One.

The rest of the witches raised their broomsticks in the air, and cackled and screeched their delight.

'Before you arrived,' said the Ancient Witch, 'Throg told me that the two girls are planning to have a midnight feast down on Femur beach. It is time for Gudrun and Hexe to prepare themselves for a very dangerous journey down into the Inside World. Now listen carefully to what I have to say.'

The Coven of witches gathered round the Ancient Witch and listened carefully as she whispered her plan on how to make Francesca and Isabella show them the way down into the Inside World.

The Ancient One said, 'Carry two of these food parcels each, and then, when the time is right, throw them to the Giant Crab for him to eat. I have mixed a magic potion with the food, which will make him feel drowsy and fall asleep.

'Then after a short time has passed by,' she continued, 'Gudrun and Hexe will be followed by two more of our sister witches to make sure that if either of the two girls should trick Gudrun or Hexe into being captured and held prisoner, they will be there to help. The two witches I have chosen to follow are Strumpel and Herika.

'I have chosen Strumpel because she is very brave, and is not afraid of anything or anybody, and I have chosen Herika because she is the cleverest of all the witches that I know.'

On that very same night, as the witches were holding their Coven, Francesca and Isabella were packing the last remaining items for their feast into a backpack.

They waited quietly for Francesca's parents to fall asleep, and when it was safe, they tiptoed down the stairs.

'We will have to leave the door unlocked for when we return,' said Isabella, 'but we should only be away for about an hour.'

'Here is your torch,' Francesca said to Isabella, 'and there is a spare packet of batteries in the backpack, should we need them.'

The two girls made their way down the winding, narrow country lane that led down on to Femur beach.

Little did they realise their every move was being observed.

Hanging from a branch high up in a tree was Basil the Bat. He had been sent by the Ancient Witch to spy on Francesca and Isabella and report back to her at the Witches' Coven when the girls left the house.

He silently left the tree and flew back to the Coven.

When the Ancient Witch heard the news that the two girls were on their way to Femur beach, she said to Gudrun and Hexe, 'It is time, my sisters, to fly down to the beach, and don't forget the parcels of food for the Giant Crab.'

Quickly, Gudrun and Hexe climbed on to their broomsticks.

The rest of the Coven cheered and cackled, 'Good luck, good luck, sisters, we shall wait for your safe return.'

The witches flew off into the night.

In the meantime, Francesca and Isabella had found a nice sheltered place on the beach, a good safe distance from the sea.

'Right,' said Isabella, 'let us unpack,' and by the glow of the full moon the two girls laid out their midnight feast.

'What time is it?' asked Francesca.

Looking at her wristwatch, Isabella said, 'we have ten minutes to go before it is midnight.'

'We shall have to wait then,' said Francesca, 'otherwise it will not be a midnight feast.'

A little way down the beach, away from the girls, two witches floated down from the midnight sky and silently landed on the beach.

'Can you see two girls over there near those rocks?' asked Hexe.

'Yes,' replied Gudrun.

'Then it is time for us to cast our Evil Spell on them,' said Hexe.

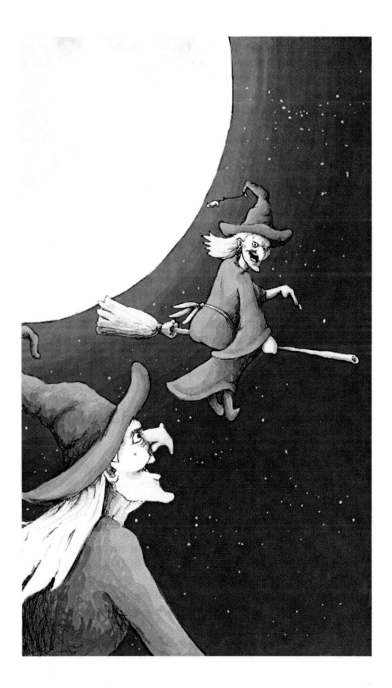

'Only two minutes to go before it is midnight,' said Isabella, looking at her watch, and at that very moment the witches cast their Evil Spell on the girls.

Pointing their long crooked and gnarled fingers at Francesca and Isabella, the witches chanted:

> By the glimmer of the witches' full moon,
> You two girls will be under our spell;
> You will obey all our orders we give you
> And will not speak until spoken to.

The two witches shuffled forward, their evil, green eyes glowing in the moonlight, and cackled with delight.

Their spell had worked, and Francesca and Isabella were now in the witches' power. If Hexe or Gudrun ordered them to do anything at all, they would obey without question.

As the witches approached Francesca and Isabella, they called out, 'Do not touch any of that midnight feast, it is for us!'

The witches dropped the food parcels that were for the Giant Crab and quickly scuttled forward, greedily gobbling down the girls' midnight feast.

'That stew which we had four midnights ago was much tastier than this midnight feast the girls have brought,' said Gudrun.

Back at the Witches' Coven in the forest, Herika and Strumpel were preparing to fly to Femur beach.

'My sisters,' said the old Crone, 'you have not much time left to help free our sister witch Koniferus. Carry this extra broomstick just in case the Nibby Nabbies have taken away our sister's broomstick, because, my sister witches, as you well know, we cannot travel without our broomsticks. It is the only way we can return to our place of never-ending moonlight.'

To the cackling cheers of the remaining seven witches, Herika and Strumpel sat on their broomsticks and flew off into the night.

On the beach, Francesca and Isabella were sitting very still and quiet. They could not make a move or a sound unless the witches gave them permission to do so.

'You girls, pick up those parcels of food for the Giant Crab, and bring your torches. Now, show us the cave that will lead us down into the Inside World.'

As they were approaching the entrance to the cave, Hexe told the girls to switch on their torches. Francesca and Isabella, followed by the witches moved slowly to the cave.

Just before they entered the cave, Herika and Strumpel arrived on the beach.

'Look,' said Herika, 'I can see two pinpricks of light over there, it has to be our sisters. We should wait a little time before we enter the cave ourselves.'

'You girls, shine your torches into the cave. Look, I can see something moving,' said Gudrun. 'It must be the Giant Crab. You, girls, take those parcels of food and leave them on the ground over there. Keep your torch lights on – crabs do not like bright lights, and he will stay at the back of the cave.'

The girls did as they were ordered.

'Now, let us return to the entrance of the cave, and wait to see what happens next,' said Hexe.

When they reached the entrance, Gudrun told Francesca and Isabella to switch their torches off again. As they waited, in breathless silence, a faint noise could be heard from within the cave.

'Switch your torches on again, and let us see what has happened,' said Gudrun.

'Look, the food parcels have gone!' said Hexe. 'We shall have to wait a little while until the Giant Crab has digested the food with the magic potions in it. When he is fast asleep we shall sneak past him, and into the Inside World.'

As they waited, a whispered voice came from the outside of the cave. 'My sisters, it is Herika. Come outside, I want to tell you something. Make sure the girls stay in the cave, I don't want them to overhear what I have to say.'

'They will not move until I give them permission to do so,' said Gudrun, 'they are still under our evil spell.'

'Well done, my sisters,' said Herika. 'Now listen carefully about what I have to say. You must tell the girls to walk down to the end of the cave first, you must not go with them.'

'Why not?' asked Gudrun.

'Because if the Giant Crab is only pretending to be asleep, he will attack the girls and devour them. If that happens, you, my sisters, will then be safe. Now go and tell the girls what they have to do, and take one of their torches away from them.'

'You are so clever, Herika,' said Hexe. 'But what will happen to us if the girls do get eaten? The Ancient One will be very angry that we have not rescued our sister, Koniferus.'

'Don't worry about that now, I will think of something. Now, go and send the girls on their way.'

Quickly Gudrun and Hexe shuffled off into the cave.

'You girls,' called Hexe. 'Go down to the end of this cave, past the Giant Crab and into the Inside World.'

Francesca and Isabella, still under the Evil Spell of the witches, did as they were ordered. After all this time since midnight, they had not spoken a word to each other.

Very slowly and quietly the girls made their way to the end of the cave, and as they approached the Giant Crab, they held each other's hands and silently walked past him and into the Inside World.

Down at the entrance to the cave, Herika said to Gudrun, 'Shine your torch to the far end of the cave, and look to see if there are any signs of the girls.'

Switching on the torch, Gudrun shone its beam down to the very end of the cave.

Francesca and Isabella were nowhere to be seen.

'It's all clear,' whispered Gudrun to the other witches, 'now let's be on our way.'

'Just a moment,' said Herika. 'The plan from our Ancient Sister is that you and Hexe go first, then after a short while, Strumpel and I will follow you, that way if there is a trap, all four of us won't be captured at the same time.'

Fearing for their lives should the Giant Crab wake up, Gudrun and Hexe, without making a sound, quietly slipped passed the Crab, and up to the wall.

'Phew, that's a relief,' whispered Gudrun. 'At least we are sure the girls are in the Inside World, now let's find the entrance.'

The witches looked all over the wall, but could not find a way in.

'Let's poke the wall with our broomsticks,' whispered Gudrun.

'That's strange,' said Hexe. 'Our sticks go through the wall as if it wasn't there.'

What the witches did not know, was that when Francesca and Isabella had entered the Inside World, as if by magic, they were no longer under the witches' Evil Spell.

'Where are we?' whispered Isabella.

'Don't you recognise it?' said Francesca very quietly. 'We are back down in the Inside World.'

'How did we get here?'

'I don't know,' said Francesca. 'Can you remember us having our midnight feast?'

'No,' whispered Isabella.

'Neither can I, we have been tricked into coming down here, but what can the reason be?'

Keeping very quiet and out of sight, the two girls continued to keep a careful watch to see if they had been followed by anything.

'I wonder what those objects are that keep poking through the wall,' whispered Isabella.

'I know what they are,' said Francesca. 'They are witches' broomsticks, and it is the witches who are responsible for you and I being down here in the Inside World. Let us keep out of sight and see what happens next.'

When the girls had entered the Inside World, they were unaware that six Nibby Nabby guards were always on duty at the secret entrance to the Inside World.

When they spotted the girls coming through the wall from their hidden vantage point, one of the Nibby Nabbies ran off down one of the many tunnels to report to the chief of all the Nibby Nabby tribes.

When the guard entered the Great Cavern, it was full of all the different tribes of Nibby Nabbies, practising their fighting skills.

When they saw the Nibby Nabby guard running up to the podium where their leader was seated, all the other Nibby Nabbies fell silent.

The Nibby Nabby guard, putting one hand over his eyes, waited to be spoken to.

Seated in the great open jaws of a long-extinct prehistoric monster was Semaj, the most feared of any leaders of the tribes that lived in the Inside World.

His face bore the scars from the many battles he had fought. His long, green dreadlocks hung down and rested on his shoulders. Around his neck was a necklace made of bones and long sharp teeth from the monsters he had slain.

In his right hand, Semaj held a double-ended trident.

On each side of the prehistoric skull, standing to attention, was a line of eight personal guards to Semaj. Each one held a single-ended trident; only the Great Semaj carried a double-ended trident.

The sixteen guards had been carefully selected because they were the tallest of all the Nibby Nabbies: each one of them stood two foot and eleven inches tall.

The fearsome Semaj, leaving his seat, looked down on the terrified guard. 'SPEAK! What have you to report,' he bellowed at the guard.

'I have grave news, Fearsome Leader,' the guard said. 'Two human girls from the Outside World have entered our Inside World through the secret wall; they have been into our Inside World before.'

'WHEN WAS THIS?' screamed Semaj.

'It happened when you were away fighting our enemies, Fearless One,' replied the guard.

Meanwhile, back at the secret wall of no return, the witches Hexe and Gudrun poked their heads through the wall.

From their hiding places, the first things Francesca and Isabella saw were two very long crooked noses with a large wart on each one.

'Those are witches' noses,' whispered Francesca. 'Let's be very quiet, try not to move, then we shall see what they get up to.'

'All I can see are lots of tunnels and piles of rocks,' said Hexe, 'and there is no sign of the girls. I think we should go back through the wall and report to Herika and Strumpel.'

'I agree,' said Gudrun.

But try as they might, it was impossible for them to go back through the wall. The only way was forward, and the two witches had now entered the Inside World.

'We must find those two girls,' screeched Gudrun, 'if we are to rescue our sister witch Koniferus. We must find them, they are still under our magic spell and will obey our orders.'

'I order you to come out from wherever you are,' shouted Gudrun.

But Francesca and Isabella stayed hidden away, for now they remembered what had happened to them and they were planning on what to do next to escape the witches and find their way out of the Inside World again.

The five remaining Nibby Nabby guards were now getting very afraid at what they were seeing.

Quietly, Number 1 Nibby Nabby guard ordered Number 4 and Number 5 guards to run down to the Great Chamber by separate tunnels.

'It will give one of you a greater chance to reach the Great Chamber, and report to our great Semaj, and tell him that two Koniferus witches have also entered our Inside World,' he said.

The two Nibby Nabbies, each carrying a trident to fight off any monsters that could be lurking in the darkened tunnels, hurried away as fast as their legs could carry them.

Nibby Nabby Number 4 ran down his tunnel, dodging from side to side across the narrow path.

The path concealed all sorts of horrible creatures that lived in the holes and crevasses of the tunnel, ready to spring out and devour anything that passed them.

The venomous tongues of the Vartrav darted out from a shallow cleft in the side of the tunnel. The Vartrav's head immediately swelled up ready for its pray. Its huge mouth was full of hundreds of sharp, barbed teeth. There was no escape from Vartrav's jaws. Running for his life, the Nibby Nabby guard missed being swallowed up by only a few inches.

Poking and stabbing with his trident at anything that tried to attack him, the exhausted Nibby Nabby guard finally reached the entrance to the Great Cavern.

Looking down, he could see all the Nibby Nabbies standing quietly to attention.

After taking a few minutes to get his breath back, the Nibby Nabby guard entered the Great Cavern. Scampering up to the podium, putting his hand over his eyes, he waited until Semaj ordered him to speak.

'What have you to report?' bellowed Semaj.

Taking his hand away from his eyes, he looked up and said, 'O, Mighty One, I have come from the wall of no return. Two witches are in our Inside World.'

'*WHAT*?' screamed Semaj. 'That's two human girls and two witches, how did they get past the Giant Crab?'

'I do not know, Mighty One,' answered the guard.

'What were these witches doing before you set off to report to me?'

'They were calling out to the girls, and ordering them to leave their hiding place, but the girls did not appear.'

Nibby Nabby Number 5 entered the tunnel he had been ordered to go down. Not a sound could be heard. Grasping his trident in both hands, and trying to avoid making any noise that would alert any predators, he very slowly walked down the tunnel. Looking from side to side he could see in the dim light hundreds of skulls and bones of past victims.

The petrified Nibby Nabby continued his silent progress down the tunnel, not knowing that there was only one predator left living in this tunnel.

After travelling for some time, at long last he saw a faint small orange glow. *That will be the end of the tunnel, the light must be coming from the Great Cavern*, he thought to himself, *I will wait until I am a little closer, and then make a dash for it.*

As the glow of light became a little brighter and larger, the Nibby Nabby, plucking up his courage, started to run as fast as he could.

Just as he got very close to the light, a huge jaw opened, and before he could stop himself, the Nibby Nabby ran down and into the wide open mouth of Dumdrol, the one-eyed ogre of the Inside World. As the Nibby Nabby slid down the throat of Dumdrol, the

ogre's mouth closed, and once again Dumdrol's single yellow eye gave off a faint glow. He could be patient and wait for his next meal. This tunnel did not have an end to it.

On the outside wall of no return, Herika and Strumpel quietly passed by the sleeping Giant Crab.

'Where are our sister witches, Gudrun and Hexe?' whispered Herika.

'We are in the Inside World,' Gudrun replied in a whisper. 'You two must join us if we are to free our sister witch, Koniferus.'

'How do we join you?' asked Strumpel.

'You must walk through the wall, but once you have touched it there is no turning back.'

At that moment, Strumpel, looking over her shoulder, noticed the Giant Crab awaking from his drugged sleep.

'We shall have to move very quickly,' said Strumpel to Herika, 'the Crab will be in a very nasty mood when he is fully awake.'

The two witches scuttled as quickly as they could through the wall of no return, and into the Inside World.

The four witches cackled their greetings to one another. Herika asked Gudrun and Hexe where the two girls were.

'They must be hiding somewhere,' said Gudrun. 'We have ordered them to obey us and come out of their hiding place, but we have not seen or heard any sign of them.'

While the witches were whispering and making plans on how to get their gnarled and crooked hands on the two girls, the remaining three Nibby Nabby guards, having seen two more witches enter through the secret wall of no return, began to tremble with fear.

'What shall we do?' asked one of the Nibby Nabbies.

'Let us make our way back to the Great Cavern, and report to Semaj, our fearless leader,' replied Number 1 guard. 'Which will be the safest tunnel to go down?'

At that very moment, the noise of a very large *BURP*! came out of the tunnel that the unfortunate Nibby Nabby had just been gobbled up in.

'We are not going down that one!' said the leader of the

guards. 'We will all go down the same tunnel, if we stick together we have a better chance of fighting any monsters that could be lurking down there.'

Francesca and Isabella were looking around for a way to escape, when Isabella spotted the three Nibby Nabby guards making their way to a tunnel entrance.

'Look over there,' whispered Isabella to Francesca, 'those Nibby Nabbies must have been watching us all the time, and it looks as if they are leaving.'

'I think we should follow them, but at a safe distance,' said Francesca.

'I agree,' said Isabella, 'but what about those four witches?'

'Fiddlesticks to them, they can find their own way out. Now, let's get out of here and get going before those Nibby Nabbies get too far in front of us, they must know the way out of here. Before we go lets look for something to defend ourselves with, let's see if we can find a strong stick for each of us.'

Then, very quickly, running from behind one rock to another, they made their way to the entrance of the tunnel, each of them picking up a stout piece of wood on their way.

'Let's hope we have not been seen by those horrible witches,' whispered Isabella.

But just as they were entering the tunnel, Herika, peering over the shoulders of her sister witches, could just see the two girls entering the tunnel with her piercing red eyes. Cackling with delight, she screeched, 'I can see those two girls entering that tunnel over there, let us follow them, I am sure they will lead us to our sister witch Koniferus.'

'Let us not be in too much of a hurry,' said Gudrun, 'if there is any danger or trouble down there, let them have it first.'

In the dim glow of light, the three Nibby Nabby guards very slowly made their way down the tunnel, each one terrified out of their wits.

After a short while, and being very careful not to be seen or heard by the Nibby Nabbies, followed Francesca and Isabella.

'Stop,' whispered Isabella, 'I think there is someone following us.'

Listening carefully, Francesca and Isabella could just hear the cackling voices of the four witches.

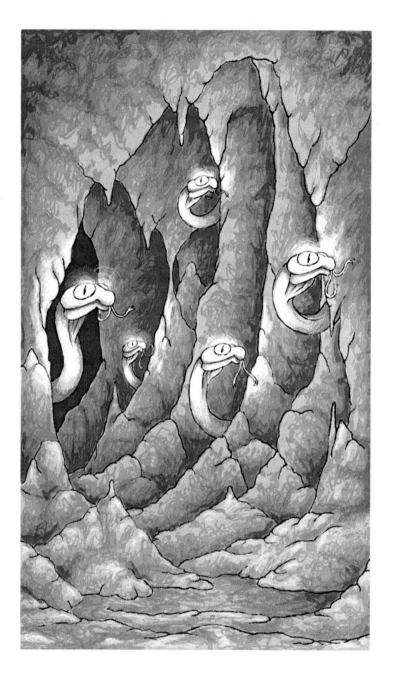

What are we to do?' asked Isabella.

Before Francesca could reply, there came the sound of a very loud scuffle; the Nibby Nabbies had journeyed into the domain of the Spittled Two-Tongued Serpents.

'We must find a place to conceal ourselves until those evil witches have gone past us,' whispered Francesca, 'but how can we do that...' she pondered.

'Look across there,' said Isabella, 'can you see that small crevice, we shall hide in there.'

'What if there are wild beasts in there?' asked Francesca.

'There is only one way to find out... come on, let's take a look.'

The two girls peered into the gloomy opening of the crevice. 'It's too dark for us to see if anything lives in there,' whispered Francesca.

Watching the two girls from inside the crevice was Old Ottler, the longest surviving creature down in the Inside World. He had a long, thin head and one eye above the other on his left cheek and a very large ear on the right cheek. He had never seen humans before, and he did not like the look of these two.

Ottler was very particular and finicky about what he ate, *I do not know where they have come from*, he thought, *but I certainly do not want to eat them; they do not look a bit tasty. I would much rather eat a juicy, one-legged Pontyprud anytime.*

Retreating further down into the crevice, Ottler watched and waited to see what the girls' next move would be.

'We shall have to chance our luck,' said Francesca. 'Come on, let's go in.'

'*PHEW*! This place stinks! I wonder what lives here.' whispered Isabella.

From their hiding place, the girls could hear the Nibby Nabbies in a frenzied battle against the Spittled Two-Tongued Serpents as they desperately fended off being touched by them. The slightest contact from a Spittled Two-Tongued Serpent would turn a Nibby Nabby into a Pontyprud and would make a tasty meal for Old Ottler. The Nibby Nabbies new this, and with great determination poked and prodded at the Serpents until they made their way out of danger.

Making their way down in to the Great Cavern, the three Nibby Nabbies quickly approached the podium, where the great Semaj was standing. They placed there hands over their eyes and waited in silence.

'You may speak,' ordered Semaj.

'Fearless One, we have just returned from the wall of no return.'

'What have you to report?' demanded Semaj.

'Great Leader,' said Nibby Nabby Number 6, 'two more witches have entered our Inside World; there are now two human girls and two lots of two witches.'

'How many does that make altogether?' shouted Semaj.

'We do not know, Fearless One, none of us can do add-up sums.'

'Well it sounds a lot to me,' said Semaj, 'I think our Inside World is being invaded.'

'What can we do?' asked the Nibby Nabby.

'We shall fight and defend our Great Cavern to the last Nibby Nabby,' said Semaj, then he ordered his personal guards to go and make sure that all the openings to the tunnels were guarded.

'Use every Nibby Nabby there is if you have to,' ordered Semaj, 'and remember there must be no sound from them once they have reached battle stations. Don't forget no fighting will begin until I give the order, now go!'

'We shall obey your command, Great Leader.'

Running down the slopes at each side of the podium Semaj's guards marched the Nibby Nabby troops to every single entrance to the Inside World.

Meanwhile, back down in the tunnel, from their hiding place, the girls could just hear the sounds of Herika, Gudrun, Hexe and Strumpel getting closer and closer.

'Shush,' whispered Francesca to Isabella. 'If we make the slightest sound they will hear us.'

And at that very moment, the four witches stopped outside the crevice.

'Did you hear that noise when we first entered the tunnel?' asked Herika, 'it sounded as if there was a lot of fighting going on.'

'It could have been those girls who have got themselves into trouble with some creatures that live down there, and if they have, I hope they have been gobbled up,' said Strumpel.

'Don't be a fool, Strumpel,' said Herika, 'we need those girls to show us the way out of this Inside World.'

Ottler, peering down the crevice could see four more from the Outside World. Trembling with fear he crept further back into the crevice to see if he could find himself a juicy Pontyprud to eat to calm his nerves.

Francesca and Isabella looked at one another across the opening of the crevice, hardly daring to breathe in case the witches would hear them.

After what seemed a very long time, they heard Herika say in a very low voice, 'Come along, my sisters, let us find where this tunnel ends, and see if we can capture those two girls. Have your broomsticks at the ready in case we should have to defend ourselves against any dangers that could be lurking ahead of us.'

Moving slowly away the four witches shuffled their way down towards the entrance to the Great Cavern.

After Herika and her sister witches had moved a safe distance from the crevice, Francesca said, 'Come on Isabella, let's get out of this smelly place and follow those horrible witches.'

As they were leaving the crevice Francesca noticed that a broomstick had been left behind by the witches.

'I will go and get it,' she said to Isabella, 'and we can take it with us. You never know, it could be very useful.'

'It looks very heavy to me,' said Isabella, 'I will help carry it.'

When the girls picked up the broomstick, not only did it weigh very little, but also Francesca and Isabella were the first people ever to have touched a witch's broomstick other than the witches themselves.

They didn't know it yet, but while they were holding the broomstick, they were given magical powers.

'Come on, let's get going, we don't want those witches to get too far in front of us,' said Isabella.

When the girls had gone, Old Ottler, with a great sigh of relief, cautiously made his way down to the entrance of his crevice. Poking his head through the opening he could see that the girls were out of sight.

Thank goodness for that, he thought to himself, *I never want to see one of those beings again.*

He settled himself down and waited for a fat, juicy Pontyprud. That would make a very tasty supper.

A long way down the tunnel, the four witches were getting closer and closer to the Spittled Two-Tongued Serpents.

Herika turned to her sister witches to see which one was carrying the extra broomstick.

'Who has the spare broomstick?' she asked.

'No one has,' said Gudrun 'we must have left it behind. I will go back and find it.'

'No, we have come too far now,' said Herika, 'let's press on and find those girls.'

The Spittled Two-Tongued Serpents could hear the cackling voices of Herika and her sister witches as they got nearer and nearer to them.

Not ever having heard such a cackling noise before, the Spittled Two-Tongued Serpents poked their heads out of the tunnel wall to see what terrible creatures could be making such a dreadful sound.

The Serpents, having lost the fight with the Nibby Nabbies, were in no mood to loose another one.

'Look down there,' said Strumpel to her sister witches, 'there are some awful-looking creatures' heads poking out from the sides of the wall.'

'Never mind,' said Herika. 'If those two girls have managed to get past them we can do the same, but make sure each of you has their broomstick at the ready, with the sharp blackthorn bush spikes pointing towards the creatures' heads.'

Having never seen witches or broomsticks before, the Spittled Two-Tongued Serpents were still ready for another battle.

'Now, my sisters,' cackled Herika, 'let us see if these Serpents will be any match for our broomsticks.'

Through the openings at each side of the tunnel, the heads of many Spittled Two-Tongued Serpents darted backwards and forwards in an attempt to get themselves a meal, but the Serpents were no match for the witches' broomsticks.

'Keep going, my sisters,' shouted Herika, 'these Serpents do not like the thorny, sharp ends of our broomsticks.'

One by one, the Serpents retreated back into their hiding places to lick their wounds.

'Well done, my sisters,' said Herika, 'now let us go and find out what type of creatures live at the end of this tunnel.'

As Herika, Hexe, Gudrun and Strumpel scuttled away from the Serpents' hideaway, in that very last moment a Serpents' head darted out and touched Gudrun's foot with one of its tongues, but before it could get its head back into the tunnel wall, its poisonous tongue dropped off and quickly wriggled away.

The evil spell, cast on them by the Ancient One to protect them from danger before the witches left the midnight Coven in the depths of Femur Forest had worked.

From a little way down the tunnel, and out of sight behind the witches, Francesca and Isabella had just seen Herika, Hexe, Gudrun and Strumpel fend off the Spittled Two-Tongued Serpents, and shuffle off down the tunnel.

'What shall we do next?' whispered Francesca.

'There is only one thing we can do,' said Isabella, 'and that is to follow those evil witches.'

'But what if the Serpents attack us?' said Francesca.

'We cannot go back, it would be too dangerous, and besides the only way out of this Inside World is to go forwards,' said Isabella.

'OK, let's get going. Keep a tight hold on the broomstick, and should any one of those Serpents poke their head out, we will bash them with our sticks,' said Francesca.

As the girls walked slowly past the openings at each side of the tunnel, they could see lots of glaring evil eyes watching their every move, but the greedy, hungry Serpents dared not attack.

They did not know how human girls tasted, and besides they had already had enough of broomsticks and Outside World creatures for one day.

When Francesca and Isabella managed to get past, and out of danger from the Spittled Two-Tongued Serpents, Francesca said, 'let's hurry and find out where those witches are.'

The girls did not know that silently following behind them, wriggled the poisonous Serpent's tongue.

As the four witches scuttled silently along the tunnel, 'Stop, my sisters!' shouted Strumpel. Pointing a long, crooked finger down the tunnel, she said, 'Look down there, can you see a bright glow?'

'Yes,' said her sister witches.

'At last,' whispered Hexe, 'that must be where this tunnel ends, but don't let us be in too much of a hurry, we do not know what lies ahead of us.'

As the witches reached the end of the tunnel, peering down into the Great Chamber, they saw hundreds of Nibby Nabbies standing in total silence.

'What are those little creatures?' whispered Strumpel to her sister witches.

'I think they are what the Ancient One was talking about before we left our midnight Coven,' said Gudrun. 'They are Nibby Nabbies, and look across there,' she said, pointing a long crooked finger towards Semaj, who was standing on the podium, 'I think he must be the leader of this tribe of Nibby Nabbies.'

'I cannot see any sign of the two girls,' whispered Herika. 'I wonder if they have been captured and taken prisoner. 'Let's hope not, we need those girls to get us out of this Inside World.'

Francesca and Isabella were standing a little distance away and out of sight behind the witches, but they could hear every word that was spoken.

In the Great Chamber, Semaj was keeping a close eye on the Nibby Nabbies to make sure that his orders were being obeyed. It was at that moment that he saw the four witches at the end of the tunnel.

'Be ready to defend our Inside World!' shouted Semaj to the Nibby Nabbies. 'The evil witches are here; we are being invaded!'

'They have seen us,' whispered Strumpel, 'what shall we do next?'

'Let's get on our broomsticks and fly around this Great Chamber,' said Herika, 'but first, my sisters, let me give each of you a bag of this magic powder,' and putting her long fingers into a ditty bag that was fastened to her skirt, she drew out three small bags of the powder, leaving one for herself.

'The Ancient One gave them to me before we left our midnight Coven.'

'What is in the magic powder?' asked Strumpel.

'Crushed bones and skins of creepy crawlies, beetles, frogs, toads, spiders, earwigs, and my favourite, eight lizard skins,' said Herika.

'But what do we use it for?' asked Hexe.

'Gather round me, sisters, and I shall whisper and tell you how this magic powder could help us to escape from this Inside World.'

From their hiding place, Francesca and Isabella could hear every word that Herika whispered to her sister witches.

Unnoticed by the girls or the witches, the tongue of the Spittled Serpent wriggled past them down into the Great Cavern.

At that moment Herika said, 'My sisters, now is the time for us to sit on our broomsticks and fly round this Great Cavern and see if we can find those two girls. I will go first, and you, my sisters, follow on after me at short intervals.'

When the last witch had flown into the Great Chamber, Francesca said, 'Come on Isabella, let's creep forward and see what is happening.'

When the girls peered into the Great Chamber, they could see and hear Semaj shouting orders to the Nibby Nabbies to do battle against the witches, who were hurtling around the Great Cavern on their broomsticks.

Amongst all the noise and chaos that was created as the witches swooped above the heads of the Nibby Nabbies, the Spittled Serpent's tongue wriggled in and out between the Nibby Nabbies.

When the tongue had touched seventeen Nibby Nabbies, turning them instantly into Pontypruds, the serpent's tongue ran out of its deadly poison, and within a few moments it had turned into an ancient fossil.

'My sisters,' screeched Herika, 'let us fly higher up, then I will tell you what we have to do next.'

When the witches reached a safe distance from any danger, their broomsticks came to a halt in mid-air.

Forming a circle, Herika whispered her plan to Gudrun, Hexe and Strumpel.

'Right, my sisters,' she said, 'let's get on with it.'

Going in different directions round the Great Cavern, they slowly flew their broomsticks over the hundreds of Nibby Nabbies, each one sprinkling the invisible magic powder over the Nibby Nabbies and Pontypruds below them, very slowly sending them into a deep, deep sleep.

Semaj, watching from the podium could see that the battle against the witches was being lost.

'Run down and see if the evil witch Koniferus is still in her cellar, and report back to me,' he shouted to the Nibby Nabby guard.

'At once, yes my leader,' said the Nibby Nabby guard, and raced off as quickly as he could.

At the end of the tunnel, Isabella said to Francesca, 'What shall we do now?'

'Let's sit on this broomstick and see what happens,' said Francesca, and before they knew it, the broomstick had carried the two girls into the Great Chamber.

'*WHOOPEE*, this is exciting,' shouted the girls as they zoomed around the Great Chamber.

'Let's land our broomstick on that podium,' said Francesca, 'I want to ask that Nibby Nabby leader some questions.'

'Right,' said Isabella.

As the girls aimed their broomstick towards the podium, Gudrun looked up and saw Francesca and Isabella gently floating down on their broomstick, and landing on the podium.

'Look over there,' she screeched, pointing a long crooked gnarled finger towards the roof of the Great Cavern, 'can you see those two horrible girls, and they are flying on a broomstick!'

'Where did they get it from?' cackled Strumpel.

'I think it must be the one we left behind,' said Gudrun.

'How can that be,' said Hexe. 'I thought those horrible girls were in front of us all the time we were in the tunnel.'

'I think they must have hidden themselves away, and let us get past them,' said Herika. 'Can you remember, my sister witches, only a short time ago at our midnight Witches' Coven, when the Ancient One warned us about how clever and quick those two horrible girls were.

'Now that all the Nibby Nabbies have been sprinkled with our magic powder,' continued Herika, 'let us stay here, then we can watch those horrible girls and see what mischief they get up to next, but remember we must be very careful and not let them out of our sight, my sisters.'

Semaj, with a look of horror and rage on his face, watched as Francesca and Isabella gently floated down and landed on the podium.

'How dare you come on to my podium!' screamed Semaj.

Before the girls could answer Semaj, the Nibby Nabby guard who had been ordered to see if the evil witch Koniferus was still locked up in her cellar, ran up to Semaj.

'What have you to report?' shouted Semaj.

'Fearless One,' said the Nibby Nabby guard, 'Koniferus the Crone is no longer in her cellar, and her broomstick is missing, and the Nibby Nabbies who were guarding her have gone, they must have run away.'

'That toothless old hell-hag must have escaped,' whispered Francesca to Isabella.

Semaj, looking around the Great Cavern, groaned in disbelief as the hundreds of Nibby Nabbies fell asleep, and thought it was time that he quickly got away, and out of the Great Cavern.

Turning to the guard he said, 'I order you not to let those girls escape, I will go down into the second Inside World, and return with reinforcements.'

'Yes, Great Leader,' said the guard, looking fearfully at the two human girls and wondering how he could possibly stop them from escaping.

Semaj walked into the huge open jaws of the prehistoric skull, and pulling on a long, razor-sharp tooth, the huge jaws quickly closed behind him, and the fearless Semaj was gone, safe away from any danger, and deep down into the second Inside World.

The poor frightened Nibby Nabby guard was left behind, the only Nibby Nabby who had escaped the witches' magic powder – the only Nibby Nabby who was not asleep.

Fearing for his life, the Nibby Nabby guard stood a safe distance from the two girls, having been told that the two girls were very brave and unafraid of anything or anybody.

Francesca and Isabella very slowly walked towards the terrified Nibby Nabby guard.

In that instant both girls shouted at the top of their voices
BOO!

The petrified Nibby Nabby guard dropped his trident and raced away down the tunnel into the second Inside World.

'Look over there,' said Isabella to Francesca, 'do you remember the last time we were down here, we escaped down that tunnel over there, and through the cave where that terrible-smelling monster guards the cascading fountain of precious stones?'

'Yes I do,' said Francesca, 'and we are going to escape the same way again. Come, let's get going, you carry the broomstick, I will get the trident that the frightened Nibby Nabby dropped, it could be very useful.'

'Good idea,' said Isabella.

Just as the two girls turned to walk off the great podium, the huge jaws of the prehistoric monster opened up, and out scuttled the evil old Crone Koniferus.

'Why are you two horrid girls down in the Inside World?' she demanded, casting her bloodshot eyes around the Great Cavern, 'and where did you get that broomstick, and why are all those hundreds of Nibby Nabbies asleep?'

'Don't you shout at us, you ugly old Crone!' shouted Francesca back at her, 'we had a spell cast on us by those horrible witches who are hovering above us,' she said, pointing the trident at the witches.

When Koniferus looked up and saw Hexe, Gudrun, Herika and Strumpel she cackled with delight. 'Fly down onto this podium my sisters, there is no danger here.'

With Koniferus's back turned to them, Francesca and Isabella took their chance to run down off the podium and towards the escape tunnel.

When the evil Koniferus turned round and saw the girls running away she screamed at them to stop and come back.

'Never, never you evil old witch!' shouted Francesca over her shoulder, as they raced away.

Koniferus knew that if the girls managed to escape, she and her sister witches would never leave the Inside World.

'Quickly, my sister witches,' screeched the evil Koniferus, 'fly yourselves down to the entrance of that escape tunnel and stop those horrid girls leaving the Inside World.'

Hexe, Herika, Gudrun and Strumpel flew their broomsticks as fast as they could, but Francesca and Isabella were far too quick for them, and ran off down into the escape tunnel.

Outside, Strumpel, in her haste to stop Francesca and Isabella escaping, lost control of her broomstick and crashed into her sister witches, bringing them down into a crumpled heap on to the floor of the Great Cavern.

'You are a clumsy fool, Strumpel' screeched the evil Koniferus from the podium, 'now wait there until I come down, and then we shall find those two nasty girls, who will show us the way out from this Inside World.'

When Francesca and Isabella had put a safe distance between themselves and the evil witches, they stopped to get their breath back.

The silence of the tunnel was broken by a strange noise.

'I wonder what is making that sound,' whispered Isabella to Francesca.

'It sounds as if something is snoring. Come on, let's go and find out what it is,' whispered Francesca.

After a short distance they came to the entrance of the cave where the fearsome Grogon lived. They saw him sitting on the cave floor with his back resting against the cascading fountain, both his chins resting on his chest, fast asleep and snoring very loudly. At his side lay a huge pile of bones, the remains of his feast.

Above the snoring of the Grogon, Isabella whispered to Francesca, 'Listen, can you hear those evil cackling witches who are following on behind us?'

'Yes I can, and we shall have to be very quick if we are to escape this Inside World and leave those nasty evil witches down here.'

Barely making a sound, Francesca and Isabella quickly made their way past the great Grogon, but they could not resist the temptation to put their hands under the cascading fountain and help themselves to a precious jewel each. Then, very quickly, Francesca and Isabella ran across and into the entrance of the escape tunnel.

'Let us stop here for a moment,' said Francesca, 'and see what happens next.'

Peering through the gloom of the Great Cavern, Francesca and Isabella could see the five evil witches looking into the cave.

'Now is our chance,' said Francesca, 'let's shout at the top of our voices and wake up that monstrous Grogon.'

'GROGON, wake up! There are five evil witches about to enter your cave.'

When Francesca and Isabella saw the Grogon wake up, they quickly ran up the tunnel and past Kroth the Keeper, and escaped from the Inside World and returned back to the Outside World.

'Let's sit down here on these rocks for a few minutes,' said Francesca.

At that moment the broomstick left her hand and flew off into the midnight sky, and back to the evil Witches' Coven.

Down in the cave, Grogon woke up to see the most dreadful sight ever, five ugly evil cackling old hell-hags standing in the entrance to his cave.

Grogon, for the first time ever, lost his courage and leapt up on to his feet and fled off down one of the many tunnels.

'My sisters,' said Herika, 'we now have to find our way out of here.'

'Look over there,' said Hexe pointing a crooked finger, 'Can you see those footprints in the sand leading towards that tunnel over there.'

'Well spotted, Hexe,' said Strumpel, 'let's go into the tunnel and see where it leads to.'

Making their way up the steep slope of the tunnel, after a short while the five evil witches were also back in the Outside World.

'Well done, my sisters,' cackled Herika, 'now let us fly ourselves back to the Coven.'

At the Coven, looking up into the night sky and against a full moon, the Ancient One could see the silhouettes of the five witches.

'Look, my sisters,' she cackled, pointing her broomstick up to the night sky, 'our four sisters have rescued our sister Koniferus, and they are all returning safely back to our Coven.'

As each of the witches flew down and gently landed at the Coven, the Ancient One and the rest of the witches shrieked their delight at the return of Herika, Hexe, Gudrun, Strumpel and Koniferus.

'Welcome, welcome back, my sisters,' said the Ancient One. 'Before you tell us what has happened this night my sisters, I have prepared a meal for you on your return to this Coven.'

'Thank you, my sisters, but before we eat I have something to add to the delicious food in the cauldron,' said Herika.

Opening her ditty bag, she dropped thirteen Pontypruds into the cauldron.

'There is one for each of us,' said Herika, 'and while they are bubbling away in the stew, I will tell you, my sisters, what has happened tonight.'

After a short time, when the Coven of witches had eaten, the Ancient One said, 'Come, my sisters, it is time for us to fly back to our land of never ending midnights before the sun rises.'

As the witches flew away into the night sky, looking down, Herika said, 'Look over there, my sisters; there are those two horrible girls who have given us so much trouble.'

'Don't worry, my sisters,' shrieked the Ancient One, shaking her fist at the two girls, 'I have not finished with them yet, we shall return and have our revenge.'

As Francesca and Isabella made their way home in the darkness, Isabella said to Francesca, 'What will you do with that Nibby Nabby's trident?'

'I will hide it in the secret place in my tree house,' said Francesca.

'Good idea,' said Isabella. 'Now, let's go home.'

Just before the girls fell asleep, Francesca said, 'Well, that's five witches who are in the Inside World and will never return to the Outside World to cause us any problems.'

Printed in the United Kingdom by
Lightning Source UK Ltd., Milton Keynes
141601UK00001B/45/P